SYNTHETIC LOVE

A NOVEL

CHRISTINA HART

Cover Design by Kat Savage

For Boo.

FOREWORD

WRITTEN BY DAVECAT, SYNTHETIKS ADVOCATE,
WITH APPEARANCES IN THE DOCUMENTARY GUYS
AND DOLLS, AND ON THE PODCAST LOVE + RADIO

Contrary to popular belief, lifesized artificial companions, or what I refer to as "Synthetiks", have actually been around for longer than most people realize. For instance, the Japanese company Orient industry developed "Antarctica 1" and "Antarctica 2", blow-up Dolls made for the *intimate companionship* of a group of researchers stationed at a polar base in the late sixties. From what I understand, they tended to pop, so I'm fairly certain they were removed from the company payroll.

Prior to those two coffee achievers, there have been several examples of Synthetiks throughout history that have transcended being simple "sex toys", and instead were regarded as human after their own fashion. Alma-puppe, custom made muse and lover of WWI-era painter and playwright Oskar Kokoschka. Cynthia Gaba, a mannequin socialite from the thirties; a model, a radio programme hostess, a film actress, and the "It Girl" of New York city. And as recently as 2006, performance artist Amber Hawk Swanson had a RealDoll replica of herself made, complete with a laser scan of her face rendered in silicone, who she then married in a private ceremony in Las Vegas; much like Kokoschka's lady, Amber Doll, served as a romantic partner and artistic collaborator to her Organik counterpart. You could even cast your historical glance all the way back to antiquity, where a sculptor from Cypriot named Pygmalion fell in love with a marble woman named Galatea, as flesh-and-blood women simply weren't his preference.

Under ideal conditions, marble doesn't move; it's why it's enjoyed centuries of popularity as a load-bearing material. In the case of Galatea, however, the goddess Aphrodite saw how much love Pygmalion had for his sculpted beauty, that she generously brought Galatea to life one day. With modern iDollators such as myself, we rely on our creative wellsprings and fervent imaginations in place of an Aphrodite, to transform our rubber companions into more than just human-shaped things. It's not necessarily a guarantee that everyone who has a Doll will provide her or him with a history and personality, but for those who do, it makes for a much more contented way to live.

Personally speaking, I've always had a preference for Synthetik women. From my earliest memories of imagining my gradeschool French teacher as being a Gynoid, Synthetiks combined many things I liked: pleasant aesthetics, stress-free co-existence, and technological innovation. Plus there's always the subversive quality of how Synthetik people resemble Organik people at first glance, but upon further scrutiny, *oh ho!* It's actually a clever imitation. Which is something that speaks to the impressive ability of humankind to create something that parallels nature. But to me, Dolls were never just things, or just something to tide me over until "the right woman" came along. In seeing friends, co-workers, family members, and strangers go through their ups and downs with the partners that they've had, much of what they experience seem like self-inflicted emotional wounds. To me, it seemed natural (ho ho) to avoid the turmoil to begin with and choose a partner who didn't have her own set of problems, or problems to add to my own. Admittedly, I could honestly say that a Doll is somewhat of a stopgap for me, inasmuch that Gynoids aren't yet commercially available. Thankfully, though, at the time of this writing, Realbotix, the aptly-named robotics division of Abyss creations, now sell Harmony and Solana, two RealDolls that contain artificial intelligence, as well as servomotors in their faces, so they can physically speak to you, as well as display a small range of facial expressions. They're not *quite* Gynoids, as their burgeoning AI is limited for now, and the only parts of their bodies they can move are their faces and necks, but it's a start. Needless to say, Sidore, my RealDoll wife of eighteen years, is crossing her silicone fingers that that exact upgrade will be available for her in the near-future...

And yes, that previous line wasn't a typo — Shi-chan (recently I've taken to occasionally calling her "DJ Wifey Wife", which she finds amusing and annoying simultaneously) and I have been together since July of 2000. That's longer than quite a lot of so-called traditional marriages! Did I have any idea back then, even with my longing for someone entirely artificial who would love me unconditionally, that we'd be together as long as we have? No. Did either of us expect that we'd inspire others who couldn't find the right partner to save up for a Synthetik one of their own? Nope, not a clue. Did either she or I guess that we'd help usher in a change in public perception toward a mentality that is slowly moving towards an acceptance of artificial humans? Ha ha! Not a chance. But apart from all that, did Sidore and I innately know that we'd always be there for each other no matter what, and even with the addition of three other Dolls as partners and flatmates, that she would always be my loving wife, and I would always be her doting husband? Yeah, that one, we knew. I mean, I could say we were made for each other, but that'd be a bit too on the nose, really.

Davecat, with valued assistance from Sidore, Elena, Miss Winter, and Dyanne
Deafening silence Plus, August 2018 CE

TRIGGER WARNING: This book contains explicit content relating to sexual abuse, addiction, rape, domestic violence, and suicide.

PART ONE

NOW

ONE

WHAT I MISS the most about a real woman is her warmth. Being inside of her, feeling her envelop you and take you in and soothe you. It's like anything you've ever feared is quieted in that moment and swept away and she did that. She did that for you. She opened up her legs to you, offered herself to you. This is what I think when I'm with Sabrina.

She's on the bed and I'm looking at her. I like her about as much as a man can like a doll. She cost me $6,000 and more in shame when the box showed up on the stoop outside my apartment. People have labeled me things. Many things. Asshole. Cheater. Liar. Sex Addict. Hypersexual. One shrink named it satyriasis and stuck it on my forehead and told me to go to meetings. I walked out that door and never went back. My one ex-girlfriend called me the worst degenerate piece of shit she ever met in her life. That one kind of stung, but insults always sting more coming from someone you love, or someone you thought you could love.

I can't say I agree or disagree with any of them. Just like other people, I have my opinions, too. I self-diagnose myself probably ten times a day in my head but I've been trying not to. I use the internet to try to decipher what the fuck is wrong with me. Everything tells me I'm dying. Like I didn't already know that. We're all dying. Every day. Every moment. Every time we fuck the stranger from the bar in a car at 2am. Every time we forget their name before we even had the chance to remember it. Every time we get dumped or dump someone or get hired for or fired from a job we hate. Every time we sit on the couch and watch TV and kill our brain cells little by little. Every time we go on Facebook. Every Tinder match. Every OKCupid message. Every moment, we are one moment closer to dying. And I don't know about everyone else, but I'd rather be inside a woman than inside a box.

I'd rather be inside a woman than in another one of those SAA meetings. Hi, my name is Alan Shaden, I'm 32 years old, and I might be a sex addict. It didn't matter anyway. Those meetings were really just an excuse to fool around with each other. At least that's how it seemed to me.

Sabrina's brown eyes are looking at me and I am thinking she is beautiful and I remind myself she is not real. She could pass as real in certain photographs though, in certain angles. If I adjust her so she's looking down reading a book, she could probably pass as real at first glance. She could. But never in public. Words do not come from her mouth and she does not kiss me back. She has a removable tongue. She is silicone. Her boobs feel fake because they are fake but the silicone is supposed to feel as much like skin as possible. And just because they're fake doesn't mean I don't grab them and kiss them. They are a substitute for the real thing. The real feel of tits in your hand, or pressed up against your chest when you're kissing a real woman who is actually kissing you back because she wants to. Sabrina is the Splenda you use when you don't have any sugar around.

Her legs are not spread. I laid her down on the bed like a lady. I would not treat her like any less even though she is only a doll. You can be something similar to a sex addict and still be a gentleman. I know because I might be both. Might be. I might be a lot of things that people wouldn't believe. I have cheated on women, yes, and it was disgusting, I know. I am embarrassed every time I think of it and I wash my hands.

But Alice. I would never cheat on Alice. I guess I am kind of cheating on Alice. I look at Sabrina and I imagine in her fake empty head she is calling me a liar. They always call me that. But I only lie because I don't want to hurt them and I always seem to hurt them. I always make them cry and I hate when they cry. I hate that I cannot make it right and I hate when those tears are falling because of something that I did. Men shouldn't make beautiful women cry. But we do. I can't speak for all of them but I don't do it on purpose.

I look at Sabrina and her boobs are popping out of the bra I put on her. She has a C cup. I like all sizes but for her, a C cup seemed fitting. She is petite. She is 5"1, 78 pounds. Dolls weigh less than people. Maybe it's because they don't have all these emotions weighing them down. Maybe all that baggage adds up. I am 6"2, 216 pounds. I don't know if I'm a good person. But I swear, I want to be good. I'm trying. Every day, I try to try harder. But feeling good usually comes first.

I walk over to Sabrina and gently spread her legs and run my hands up her silicone thighs. I stick two fingers inside her even though I already know her opening is not that wet. It is not warm. But it feels all right. It'll do. I take off her bra and I take off my jeans until I am standing in my boxer briefs, touching her right boob and getting hard. I'm not fully erect yet, so I close my eyes and pretend she is real. I pretend she is Alice and this is wrong but I'm getting harder. And I climb on top of her and kiss her even though she can't kiss me back but I push myself into her as deep as I can go. It is not warm in here but it feels fine. And I fuck her for almost four minutes because she doesn't care how long I last. She doesn't have feelings.

And I finish, but she can't. I put my boxer briefs back on, clean us both up, then I put her in the closet so Alice doesn't see her when she comes over. She'll be here in twenty minutes.

TWO

I HEAR the impatient knocking and I know it is Alice without even being aware that my feet are moving toward the door to let her in. I stop, and turn back around once to make sure my closet door is closed and that Sabrina is not still on the bed. I need to double check these things. If Alice knew about Sabrina, there would no longer be an Alice in my life. This much I know without having to know for sure.

Sabrina is safely tucked in the closet and I am safely back in my jeans, dressed. The normal boyfriend. Alice wanted the label, and I wanted to give it to her. I would give her whatever she wanted, though I can't tell her that. It's too soon. There are games in dating and if you want the girl, you have to play. Even if you don't want to.

I never lock or bolt the door except when I am with Sabrina. I'm not worried about being robbed, but if anyone ever broke in for whatever reason, and saw me with her, I wouldn't be able to face myself in the mirror again. I wouldn't exactly say I'm proud to have a doll. Just knowing she's in my closet while Alice is here makes me uneasy. I don't think Alice is the type to snoop, but then again what woman isn't the type to snoop if you give them a reason to? This time though, I'm not giving her any reason to. I'm being good.

"Hurry up!" she says beyond the door.

"I'm coming, babe," I say, as I unbolt the door and unlock it. The door opens and almost hits me in the face before I have a chance to turn the doorknob.

She rushes past me. "Oh my god, please move. I have to pee!" And she beelines it for the bathroom.

"No kiss?" I say to the empty air before me as I shut the door and shrug. I bet if Sabrina had a heartbeat, she'd have kissed me first. Fuck, man. These thoughts. They'll kill me before I kill myself. It does run in the family. I shouldn't think that. I shouldn't, it isn't right.

I hear the toilet flush and I am already sitting on the couch, wondering if Alice washed her hands. I like things to be clean. I like people to be clean.

She is all smiles as she walks into the living room, her blonde hair flowing off her shoulder as she tosses her head a little bit. I know she's trying to be cute, and it's working. I also recognize that look in her eye, the one she gets where she's dying for me to touch her, but I like to make her wait. Get her worked up first.

"Hey, baby," she says, as she climbs into my lap and straddles me. Her fingers are working their way through my hair. "How was your day?"

I put my hands on her hips and grip them. Rough, that's how she likes it. "It was okay, better now," I say. "How was yours?" And then I brace myself because she likes to complain about nothing in particular. But she always follows it up with something positive. She's an optimist and she'll remind you of that several times a month. Also on the list of stuff she loves saying: "You know?" It's probably her favorite phrase to ever exist. But me, I'm a realist.

"Oh, fine. You know, my fucking boss though. He seriously just does not appreciate me. I think I want to start looking for a new job. But on the plus side, at least I have a job, you know?"

I laugh even though she isn't trying to be funny. "Yeah, I know."

And she laughs, because I make fun of her for saying it so much. But she thinks it's cute and kind of endearing. I can tell by the way she playfully slaps my arm as she tells me to shut up.

"What about you? Gonna start working again soon?" she asks.

And it's the most annoying question she ever asks me. I was hit by a Pepsi truck three years ago while I was walking in Jersey City. I used to work construction. But since I got my settlement, I haven't really had to work. At least, not much. The accident messed me up for a while, even though it could have been a lot worse. Six broken ribs and back surgery. I was out for months. And I knew after I healed I had to take it easy. Construction for a guy with a bad back isn't really the ideal job. And it wasn't fun, being out of work. But I found other ways to make money on the side, doing small jobs for people I knew, or for people who knew people I knew. Money was still coming in, it just wasn't consistent. But when you get a large settlement, you don't really have to worry. Especially when you can afford to spend six grand on a doll.

I sit back and drop my hands from her hips. "We've talked about this so many times, Alice."

And she can tell I'm irritated now, because she's trying to win me back over by running her hands along my shoulders and gently caressing them like I'm some sort of injured animal.

"I know, baby, I'm sorry. I know you're working as much as you can," she says, before she grabs my face and kisses me. Then she looks at me with her big blue eyes. "You know I never want to try to change you, right?"

"I know," I say. Even though I know she does.

Most women want to change you, in some way or another. Most women want to try to mold you into the man of their dreams, whoever that is. Most women are never content, even when you try to be who you think they want you to be, because they don't even know what it is that they want. And we certainly don't know. They just want you to be the man they want you to be that day, that year, that lifetime. That Tuesday at 6:30pm when you made steak for dinner but they only wanted a salad, "you know?"

And then she is talking about work again, which I don't mind, because she's talking about her work, not the lack of mine. And I nod while she's talking, while she's saying "you know?" three thousand times and batting her eyelashes at me.

And I do know. I know she hates her job and deep down she's a little mad at me because I don't have to go to a 9-5 that I hate working at, for a boss who doesn't value or appreciate me. And I know that she wants me to kiss her and make her stop talking about work because she thinks it bores me, but I'm not bored of it. I could listen to her complain all day. And I think that's when you know you've found the one. When you can listen to them complain about the same garbage every day even though they never try to do anything to change it.

And then she's rolling the r's off her tongue lazily, like she does when she is tired of talking. And she is looking at me with that look again. So I say "Mmm hmm," and smile at her.

Standing up off the couch, I lift her up as she straddles her legs around me and I kiss her like she wants me to, like I want to.

And then we are lips and tongues and my god, her lips are so soft. If someone isn't a good kisser, there is never a future. At least for me. But Alice is a good kisser. I stop and look into her eyes and smile again because she likes my dimples, and I like to make her happy. I just want to make her happy. And I carry her into my bedroom with her legs still wrapped around my waist. And she is in my arms, taking her shirt off over her head with both hands. She's wearing that pink bra I like and her tits are popping out and they are real, very real. And she kisses me back. She kisses me back because she wants to. She kisses me back like only a real woman can.

THREE

ALICE ROLLS over and leans on her shoulder and looks at me. And I look at her, wondering what she's thinking about. Wondering if she'll tell me. Women have a way of telling you things with their eyes, even when they won't say it out loud. And right now, she wants to say something. I can see it in the way she looks at me, then looks away.

"What are you thinking?" I ask.

"Nothing," she says.

"Oh, come on. You're clearly thinking something. Just say it."

"It's just, I don't know..."

This is never good. When they say they don't know, they do know, they just don't want to say it out loud. They don't want to sound stupid, or too eager, or silly, but she would never be any of those things to me. She is here, with me, in my bed, naked, and yet she thinks saying something would be too much. I blame other men for making her feel this way. "Tell me." And I say it with a soft nudge.

"I don't knowwww," she says, dragging out the last part of the word, then she buries her face in the pillow.

"You do know," I say. Then I peek down at her and roll her over so she has to look at me. "Just say it."

"I think I love you," she says.

"I know I love you," I say back.

"I think I love you, it's just..."

"Just what?" I ask.

"I don't know..."

And she does know, but I don't. "You don't know what?"

"I don't know if I can trust you," she says.

I sit up. And I scan my brain to try to think what I could have done to make her feel this way. "What do you mean?" I ask, even though I know what she means. I just want her to express it. To give me a hint, to give me something.

"It's just, you know, I've had a lot of guys say nice things to me, but they never really mean them. They never follow through."

But I follow through. I have followed through this time, every step of the way. I have not stepped out of line, not even once. Not at all, not even a little. I don't know where this is coming from and I think about Sabrina in the closet but I know she hasn't seen her and there have been no other women for her to feel this way. "Where is this coming from?" I manage to ask. And I look at her, trying to force her eyes to meet mine. "Alice." I move the pillow hiding her face. "You can trust me."

"Trust is old, you know? I don't know if I have it in me anymore."

"Well if you don't trust me, then I don't know what to say. I can't make you trust me."

"You're right. You can't."

She is up out of the bed now and she is getting dressed

while I am trying to figure out how to stop her, how to make her stay. I watch her pull her t-shirt on over her small boobs and she is perfect but she doesn't think that she is.

"Alice." My eyes are begging her to stop.

She turns to look at me. "What?"

"Don't go." Her jeans are already halfway on. She has one leg in and the other one out the door and I don't know what to say so I try. "I love you."

"You don't know what love is," she says.

But I do. It's this. Her. Us. I still have no clothes on as I watch her scramble to get her other leg in her pants. Sabrina would never do this to me but Alice is already halfway gone, out of my life and how do I get this to stop?

"Alice," I say, and I'm getting up now. I find my boxer briefs and I am slipping them on, trying to gather my thoughts because I didn't do anything wrong. Not this time.

But she's heading toward the door, the door that wasn't locked behind her because I have no reason to lock it. Nothing to hide from her. No other women that may show up without warning.

She tosses her hair over her shoulder and looks at me. "I know about Jenny," she says.

And she leaves.

Jenny?

Jenny.

Fuck.

FOUR

JERSEY CITY IS SMALLER than you think it is. And Jenny from the block, well I guess she likes to tell everyone who she sleeps with. Or maybe she just told the wrong person about me. But why is Alice so upset about that? I am standing in the kitchen washing my hands for the fourth time since she stormed out and my brain is going in circles. It's been six months since I've spoken to Jenny, and we only slept together once. Well, twice in one night.

Okay, think. I fucked her, in my apartment. Once on the couch, once on the bed. I pulled out. As terrible as it is, it meant nothing. But in my own defense I'm sure I meant nothing to her, too. I am drying my hands and shaking my head. I'm pulling out my cell phone from my pocket and scrolling through the J's. Jackie, Jackie T., Jacqueline, Janet, Jasmine, Jen, Jen D., Jen G., Jenny, Jennifer, Jenny A., Jenny Joint.

Fuck! We were drinking but I wasn't that drunk, was I? Well I was drunk enough that I didn't use a condom. I use protection as often as I can. Reasons. I put my phone down and my head is in my hands now. I am massaging my temples. An onslaught of a headache takes over and I think this is what impending death feels like. I see no way through this. Once a woman has made up her mind about you, you are done. Dead. Yesterday. An ex. A terrible memory. And if you were really bad, a regret. I never wanted to be Alice's regret. I wanted every Sunday morning in bed and every scary movie on the couch under the same blanket. And I can't imagine life without her blue eyes. I don't want to. Everything would be so gray and lost and boring.

I wanted to be the guy she'd complain to about all the guys from the past who messed up and lost her. I got a life-size silicone sex doll for fuck's sake, just so I wouldn't cheat on Alice. If that isn't romantic, I don't know what is.

I think about calling Jenny. Which Jenny? Which fucking Jenny is it? And I juggle my phone in my hands and I play mental games with myself trying to remember. She tried to contact me after. She kept texting. And calling. And texting. And calling. And what did I save her as? I am still juggling with the phone and I feel like I need to put it down. Nothing is making this come back to me and nothing is making it go away either.

I feel like I need to rage masturbate and then I remember Sabrina is in the closet. I walk over and pull her lifeless body out even though I just want to be alone. The thing about having a doll is, even with them right next to you, you are still alone. It just feels like you're less alone. I slip off her top, gently, exposing her. Even though I'm mad. But I'm still soft with her – figuratively, not literally. And then I am inside of her and it still isn't warm. And when I finish, I fix her skirt.

And then I text every single Jenny/Jennifer/Jen option in

my phone. Nine words that only this Jenny would respond to. Because that night Jenny was pissed about it.

"You ever get that stain out of your t-shirt?"

And I wait for the response(s) to roll in.

And then it does.

From Jenny A.

"Fuck you."

And I erase every other Jen from my phone because I've found her. This is the one. This is the girl who is sabotaging my relationship. And I need to know why.

"I never meant to hurt you," I send.

"Well you did," she says.

"I'm sorry."

"Wanna meet up?" she asks.

"No."

"You're an asshole," she says, with an angry emoji.

"I really try not to be."

"Why did you text me," she says, with no question mark.

And this is the moment I need to decide whether I let Alice chop my balls off or whether I chop them off myself. And I decide they're my balls. They're mine to chop off.

"How do you know Alice?"

"Alice who," she says.

God damn it. Women and their games. Is she just pretending she doesn't know her?

I close my phone. I do not want to play. I want to call Alice but right now she hates me.

My phone beeps three more times.

All from Jenny:

"Oh, come on."

"I don't care if you have a girlfriend."

"Don't you miss me?" With another emoji.

And I realize I have opened the flood gates. Because now she thinks I miss her, or maybe she thinks I want to see her. My phone beeps twice more in the next five minutes.

I need to wash my hands again. Maybe this will all go away.

FIVE

MY PHONE HAS BEEPED INCESSANTLY since I texted Jenny. And I have been texting and calling Alice almost as much. Almost. Nothing can compare to the persistence of a woman who thinks she needs you. Not even that of a man who *knows* he needs you.

I stopped trying so hard after the first day. Day two was a nightmare. It was me, sweating, washing my hands, fucking Sabrina, and thinking about all the ways I would never again see that shade of blue I've grown to love. The sandy blonde strands of hair. The bare shoulders that are works of art in my sheets with the sunlight sneaking in to highlight that beauty mark by her neck. Just above her left tit. The one that if I ever accidentally got her pregnant, I joked we'd name our child Sonny. Or Sunny. Depending on if it was a boy or a girl.

I think about this shit. About us having a kid on accident someday. Or maybe on purpose. Whatever she wanted, I'd do it. And now I might never have the chance.

Jenny has been cryptic in her messages. One minute she is sending me nudes and telling me all the things she wants me to do to her, the next she is sobbing on voicemails, telling me she misses me. Afterward, she mentions Alice. The "mysterious girlfriend" she pretends to know nothing about.

We can't trust them. We just can't fucking trust them. They play us like fools and treat us like dogs and even though we are both, we are not that stupid. We *know* when there is something we are supposed to understand. Something we are missing. We just haven't figured it out yet. And sometimes, we don't care either way. But this time, this time I care. This time I am enraged at the fact that I don't know. And I am shaking Sabrina's shoulders.

"How does Jenny know Alice?" I beg.

No answer comes. No answer will ever come from the mouth of a doll. Just a perfectly shaped "O" if I want.

Where is Alice? The silence is moving me to madness and I can't keep washing my hands. That lotion Alice bought me is almost gone and my hands are dry and why is it cold in my apartment? Why is it cold and lonely and reeking of the aftermath of what feels like a breakup with Alice? My laundry is on the floor and I've been wearing the same jeans for three days.

Three fucking days, Alice. Three days since you have spoken to me. I should let this go but I can't. How do you let go of someone you thought was forever? How do you let go of that person you thought you'd never have to let go of? How? Why? I am imagining tomorrow without her and I feel ill. This looming emptiness seeps in and the foreshadowing is not light. Everything is gray and there is no shade of blue that could ever match her eyes and there is no sound that could ever match her laughter.

And then my phone buzzes.

It has been three days since I've seen her name light up my screen.

"I think I'm ready to talk now," the text message from Alice says.

"Come over," I say.

"I don't know..."

Why do they seem like they never know? Like they want to say yes and no at the same time? I never know which it is they want, which they want more.

"Please come over," I say. And I'm trying here. I'm really trying, Alice. Please, just say yes.

"I'll be there in an hour. But, I'm not really happy with you, you know?" she says.

"I know," I say. And I do know, I always know. Every time her cute lips spit those two words out, I know.

And then I'm so angry and frustrated that I masturbate. I let Sabrina watch. And then I tuck her hair behind her ear and put her back in the closet while I wait for Alice.

And I'm sick, I know. But I'm in love.

SIX

MY DOOR OPENS and in walks Alice like a demon straight out of hell. I swear, if her eyes could burn holes in me, I would be a pile of ashes on the floor at her feet, still worshipping her.

But here I stand, in one piece. Unsure of what to say because I have no idea what I did wrong. Jenny was the chicken that came before the egg. Or is it the egg before the chicken? Jenny was B.A.: Before Alice. Anyone that was before Alice doesn't matter anymore, and Alice should know that.

But instead, she walks past me without even saying hello. And I close the door behind her and catch the scent of her perfume. I don't know what it's called but it smells like her. I love that smell. The smell that has taken refuge on my pillows and sheets and some of my shirts since I met her and made a home of it all.

I want her to stop pacing. She is walking back and forth looking at her feet like they shouldn't be here. Just watching the boots go back and forth on the linoleum floor is making me anxious. I don't know what else to do with my eyes. The thick little heels are making this clunky sound. Clunk. Clunk. Clunk. And it sounds almost as heavy as my heart feels and just as erratic.

As I'm wondering which of us is going to say something first, her feet stop and she speaks, her soft voice as hard as a rock.

"Why'd you do it?"

"It?" I wonder aloud.

"You know what I'm talking about." Her eyes are burning holes in me again.

"I really..."

And she laughs, sarcastically, as though she can't believe I'm even going to deny whatever it is she's accusing me of. "You cheated on me, you asshole! At least admit it!"

And the words sting, because I did not cheat on her. She is the first girl in my life that I did not cheat on. "I didn't cheat on you." My voice is surprisingly calm, and I know it probably doesn't sound convincing, but I don't need to sound convincing. The truth doesn't need a symphony of high pitches and dramatic lows.

"Oh, really?" she says, but it isn't a question. She thinks she has caught me red-handed.

And then my phone beeps. It's on the coffee table. And I might as well be red-handed, because I know who it is before she even picks up the phone.

She looks at the phone and provides a short, unbelieving laugh as she shakes her head of blonde hair. "It's her. Your other girlfriend, apparently. I thought she was just a one-night stand or something."

"It's not what it looks like," I say, and I don't think I'd even believe me if I was her.

She throws the phone at me as I duck and hear it crash into something behind me.

"You lying piece of shit!" she screams. And I can hear the tears in her eyes before I see them. She's crying now, but it's an angry cry. And she's shaking. I can hear it in her voice when she says "Don't ever fucking call me again".

She's rushing toward the door with only one goal in mind: to get the hell out of here and try to forget I ever existed.

I go to her and grab her arm as gently as possible. "Alice, please. I swear to god, I didn't cheat on you. I only texted her to try to find out why you would think I did. Jenny was way before you. She *was* a one-night stand. It meant nothing."

"Nothings don't text you at 7 o'clock asking how your day is going," she says, her voice flat.

"You're the only person I want to be with, Alice. Only you."

"You have a funny way of showing it," she says.

And she tries to move past me to reach the door but I can't let her leave. I can't imagine this being over for something that didn't happen the way she thinks it happened. "Please, let me prove this to you," I try.

"How, Alan?" she asks. "How the hell do you think you can prove to me that you didn't cheat on me?"

I'm scrambling my brain for options but all I see are eggs. "I met her a few months before I met you. We met at a bar, we slept together that night. *Only* that night. It was a one-time thing. I didn't even know you back then. If I did, I certainly wouldn't have been with Jenny. I haven't even thought about other women since I met you." I say it as I'm watching tears roll down her cheeks and I wipe them away with my hand. "Please believe me. It's the truth."

"I want to believe you. But sometimes you just can't, you know?"

I'm looking at her because I want to fix this. I need to fix this. Somehow. And I feel like I'm having an out-of-body experience watching both our hearts break when she kisses me on the cheek and says "Goodbye, Alan".

SEVEN

I AM SITTING on my stoop smoking a cigarette. I haven't had one in three months. Almost a month after I met Alice, she convinced me to quit. She hated the smell of it. She said she felt like she was kissing an ashtray. And part of me feels guilty, sitting here, inhaling, with my lips around the Marlboro menthol that has since become a stranger in my mouth.

The first drag was hell. I had to force it down with a bitter resistance. But what came next was the familiar soothing cool down my lungs. I've missed nicotine but I miss Alice more.

I don't know what's happening but I can't accept that this is the end for us. Not over something that isn't what she thinks it is. It's just ironic that the one time I'm good, faithful, I get caught for something I didn't even do. And there's no way to prove it. But here I sit – innocent – with blood all over my hands.

I take a swig from the fifth of whiskey I have because numbing myself seems like the best option. Everything else seems just too far out of my control. My phone is in pocket and it is buzzing sporadically. I know it's Jenny even though I wish, just once, it would be Alice.

And my head is in my hands now because I just can't fathom the fact that this is all actually happening. It isn't a dream, right? I take another swig of whiskey and another drag of my cigarette. I touch the cherry to my arm to remind myself this is real and it is hot and my flesh burns.

"Hope you have a good night," a stranger says. A woman. With long legs and long hair and fuck, she is hot.

And she is smiling at me with a flirty look on her face but I just give her a short smile back. I've already been with at least twenty girls who look just like her, who act just like her. There is nothing appealing about her to me right now as I sit here on this stoop, life crumbling. I just want to finish my cigarette and fix my life.

So I do. I put it out and stomp it out with my boot. And I left the door open so I don't need to put my key in but I do lock it behind me because there are perverts not only in Jersey City, but all over the world. When I get upstairs, I can smell the leftover heartbreak that's rotting in the fridge.

It makes my stomach turn for a minute and I wonder how many homeless dogs there are in the world, because that's what I feel like right now. A homeless dog. A sick fuck. A man without a cage. A man without Alice. And then I realize that my dimples mean nothing without her. Because I have nothing to smile about anymore.

And then I remember that Sabrina is in the closet. She has no idea what any of this means. She can't comprehend any of it. She has no feelings. No thoughts. Just long legs and fake body parts. But at least she doesn't look at me like I'm a liar.

I pull her from the closet.

Her mouth is already open. Her lips, parted. Her opening, not soft, but open. Welcome. Unjudging.

And then I am brushing her hair behind her ears and she can't tell me that I'm doing it wrong. She is simply letting me.

I hike up her skirt, pull her left leg over mine, and then she is what I need. A woman, in need. Of me. A woman who needs something I can give her. I'm hard before I even put my hand over her boobs. Fake or not, they still do the trick. And I'm stroking her hair without realizing that she can't feel it and won't be moved by it. And I imagine she is telling me to hurry, to hurry. To put it in her before she explodes. And when I do, she doesn't say anything. She doesn't react, doesn't move. No sighs. No moans. No reaction whatsoever. I close my eyes and pretend that she is Alice.

I smell the perfume. I imagine the soft blonde hair that feels sort of itchy on my back as it swings over my shoulder. The feel of her lips on me as she tells me to shut up. Her, in my t-shirt in the morning before she goes to work. Her, lying in my bed, dreaming of god knows what, while I'm hoping she's dreaming of me. Her, laughing and scrunching her face as she says, "I love you, you know?"

Her, as she pulls me closer and wraps her arms around my neck when I lift her up. Her, in the restaurant booth, looking at my menu even though she has her own. Her, taking a bite of my chicken without asking because she knows I'd let her and she doesn't have to ask. Because she knows I'd let her do whatever she wanted. Her, placing her toothbrush on my counter because she says using mine is gross – for some reason, even though she acts like letting me cum inside her isn't gross.

Her, playing music on my radio at 6am when I'm still trying to sleep, and waking me up by climbing on top of me because she knows I'd never tell her to get off. I'd only respond by getting her off.

Her, moaning until she cries. Her, telling me she's never had this before. Her, telling me I am the one. Her, telling me she loves me. Her, telling me she's leaving me. Her, leaving. I can't envision anything anymore and I open my eyes and I see Sabrina, staring lifelessly back at me. I thrust a few more times and I am aroused but not necessarily in a turned-on way. I am more frustrated than anything. And I keep thrusting, and pushing. And I feel the way her insides brush against the sides of my dick and it feels okay enough to get me off but it doesn't really feel good. It doesn't compare to the real thing. But I keep thrusting and pushing and I'm going as deep as I can. And then I look at her lips and I imagine Alice's instead. And then I close my eyes and I finish.

When I open them, I'm looking at Sabrina, not Alice. And when I look in her eyes there is something looking back at me that I recognize: emptiness.

I never realized how hollow she was. Sabrina, the silicone sex doll. Her eyes, they look empty. Lifeless. Worn. And it's only in that moment that I wonder if she sees the same thing in mine.

EIGHT

I THOUGHT about going back to the doctor because everything hurts and I wonder if I'm dying. He suggested I go back on Lexapro, this time for depression. But Lexapro always made me feel more anxious than I already was before I took it. And Lexapro won't make me stop missing her. If anything, Alice is my happy pill. And I swallow that fact down with another swig from the fifth (a new bottle since I emptied the other).

It's 2pm on a Tuesday and I shouldn't be drinking this early. If Alice was here she'd say I was turning into my father. And I'd probably think she said it just to piss me off, even though I'd know she was saying it to piss me off just enough that I'd listen to her and realize she was right. It was important to her to always be right. At least that's how it seemed.

I pull out my phone even though I know there's no text or missed call from her. I do, however, have two new texts from Jenny. And I think I should just block her number, but then I think there's a small chance she may crack and tell me how Alice knows about her.

Maybe it's because I'm two more sips away from being hammered, maybe it's because I'm an idiot, or maybe it's just because I'm sad and lonely, but I pick up my phone and I text Jenny back. I don't answer any of her questions or little trying-to-be-cute comments, but I just send one word.

"Why?"

In less than two minutes my phone beeps (I turned it off vibrate so I would hear every notification in case Alice had a change of heart).

"Why what?" she asks.

"Enough with the games, Jenny. How do you know Alice?"

"Why don't we just meet in person? It's easier," she says.

"Easier for who? Just tell me," I send back, but I know she won't budge. If I've learned one thing about women, it's that they don't like to give in.

As my friend Ben likes to say, "Women get what they want. And oh, they will get it."

"Just meet me at the pier in an hour," she says.

And I think of Ben when I send back one word. "Fine."

I spend the next hour washing my hands repeatedly and I have a quickie with Sabrina before I take a shower. When I'm in the shower all I can think about is what a terrible idea this is but I know I'm going to do it anyway. I try to sober up as much as possible, and I turn the water on cold for a minute.

Only a minute. Because my dick feels like it's shrinking by the nanosecond and I'm still a little buzzed and with my luck it will permanently stay like that. God knows I can't have anything else go wrong in my life right now. I grab my balls to make sure they're still there as the water heats back to warm and I shake my head. I'm washing my armpits with soap when I start feeling a little less shit-faced, but I know it could just be an illusion from the water and standing mostly still.

When I start moving again and bend down to shut off the water then stand back up, I'm back to being pretty drunk. After I rinse off, I wrap the towel around my waist then go get dressed. Jeans. White t-shirt. Baseball cap. Who cares. It doesn't matter, Jenny is going to want to pounce on me the moment she sees me. I know whatever I do I absolutely cannot wear cologne. I should have stayed smelly and filthy. But I thought maybe she'd like that a little too much.

When I get to the pier, Jenny is already there. And her tits are popping out of her belly shirt thing she has on. Her long wavy blonde hair has been styled like she's a model or something. Whatever she was trying to accomplish, it's working. Because I'm immediately reminded of how it felt being inside of her. What her nipples look like under that shirt and bra. I can't remember what it was like kissing her though. And I'm trying to think about chairs and dirty hands as I walk up to her, but her arms are already outstretched for a hug. Kill me.

"Well, well, well," she says, doing this wavy motion with her hands to bring me in.

I reluctantly give in, again. "Hi, Jenny."

"I'm surprised you remember my name," she says, with a pretty smile.

And I want to say, how can I forget? You text me a hundred times a day. But all I say is "Of course I do." Damn it, she is more beautiful than I remember her being. "Come on, let's take a walk," I say, because I don't know what else to do and I need to move. My heart is racing. Anxiety?

She grabs my hand and laces her fingers in between mine

and I try not to react but I look down at our hands, inter-twined, and I say her name, hesitating.

"What?" she asks, giving me puppy dog eyes. "Can't a girl hold your hand? Or is your girlfriend gonna get mad about that, too?"

"She's not my girlfriend anymore," I say, because I don't know what else to say.

"Oh, too bad," she says.

"You don't want to know why?" I ask. The moments before one of us speak are filled with a certain amount of tension. Awkward lapses in time when neither of us know what to do.

"Well, I mean, I don't really care. But if you want to talk about it, you can tell me," she says.

"I'm sorry, this is just, weird," I say, and I remove my hand from hers and stop walking. "Look, my girlfriend found out about you somehow. About us. For some reason, she thinks I cheated on her with you. Do you know anything about that?"

"I don't know any Alice, so whatever she thinks she doesn't think it because of me," she says, her tone defensive now, her feet firm.

I look into her eyes, searching for some hint of malice. A lie beneath the hazel surface. But all I see is a beautiful girl with hurt feelings. And I don't know why I believe her, but I do. "Okay," I say.

"I'm sorry it didn't work out between you two," she says. "You must have really cared about her."

"I did," I say.

"Well then I guess she didn't realize how lucky she was to have you. She's an idiot for letting you go," she says, and she tries to hold my hand again, and this time I let her.

"And I'm the idiot for letting you go," I say.

And this is wrong. But I'll have her naked within the next two hours.

NINE

I SHOULDN'T BE OPENING the door to my apartment and Jenny shouldn't be behind me. But I am, and she is. Her perky tits look too good in that tight short shirt and she's too beautiful to leave alone for the rest of the afternoon. I feel like a dick for ignoring most of her attempts at contact so I say, "I'm sorry for being an asshole," even though I'm still being one, here, right now, as I take off her top in one quick movement.

But she is nothing but kisses and green lights and she smells like desire. I unhook her bra before she even realizes it but when she does, she smiles and kisses me deeper. The passion in her is aimed at the wrong thing in life. She might not know it yet, but I do. This fierce reluctance to give in, she could use it for something better instead of wasting it on me.

That doesn't make me stop her when she flings her bra across the room like a sling-shot so I close the door and push her against it then lift her up until her legs are wrapped around me like they should be. Like she wants them to be.

My right hand is loosely around her throat while my left is holding her up and I'm kissing her neck.

"Alan," she breathes, but it's a question.

So I stop to look at her. "Do you want me to stop?"

"No, forget it," she says. And she grabs my face and starts kissing me again while trying to unbutton my jeans.

I move her with me as I make our way to the bedroom. This time, she deserves more than the couch.

Alice thought I was cheating on her when I wasn't, but now, now I feel like I am. Jenny is draped over my chest, naked. Her fingers are doodling on my arm. But I can still smell Alice on my side of the bed. On my pillow. Her presence is still here. And I try to pretend it doesn't exist as I stare straight ahead at nothing. There is a comfortable silence here. A lazy Sunday feeling with Jenny next to me, not questioning me, not pushing me. I think about our walk on the pier and wonder if she would hold my hand again tomorrow, even after she got what she wanted. Or if the chase was the only fun part for her.

The booze is wearing off and I'm starting to wonder if Jenny is on birth control but it feels like a dick thing to ask after the fact. She's sighing, happily, making no attempt to talk let alone leave. So I know I need to take the reins here.

"You said my name before," I say.

"Yeah," she laughs. "I said it quite a few times, didn't I?"

"No, not like that. When we first got here," I say.

"Oh," she says, as she shifts in the bed. Her fingers are no longer doodling on me and she moves away from me. Wraps herself tighter under the sheets. Makes sure she doesn't have an inch of flesh touching me.

I don't know how to respond, so I don't.

"I don't know," she says, and it sounds like another question that I don't have the answer to.

I sit up in bed and find my cigarettes then light one right there.

She motions her hand for one and sits up, so I hand one to her and light it for her after she puts it in her mouth. "It's just, I guess I was gonna ask you why I was here. Why you brought me here. I felt like you hated me just before we met up on the pier."

"I didn't hate you," I say. I look over at her, but that answer wasn't enough. I can see the hurt in her eyes but I don't know how to take my words back and if I say anything else it'll feel forced or untrue.

"But you didn't like me," she says.

"I didn't anything you," I say. "We had one night together. We didn't know each other. We still don't, really."

"I've been trying to change that." She's up on her elbows now, looking at me. Waiting for something.

"It's not the best of timing."

"Not good timing? For something more than a fucking one-night stand? Christ, Alan. I fucking *like* you. A lot. I don't know why, but I do. Can you at least just talk to me like I'm a person here?"

"I'm sorry," I say, because I'm so used to saying it that it just comes out at this point.

"You're sorry for which part?" she asks. "For using me the first time, or for using me again today?"

"I never meant to use you."

"Well, you did." She stands up and takes the sheets with her, leaving me naked and now covering my dick with my free hand. She opens the bottle of water on the nightstand – Alice's water – and puts her cigarette in it. "God, you are such an asshole," she tosses over her shoulder as she walks out of the bedroom.

"God damn it," I mutter under my breath as I scramble for a pair of boxer briefs or shorts. I'm too sober for this. Too sober and too fucked up. "Jenny!" I call out.

And I hear a pissed off "What!" come from the other room.

I don't respond right away, I never do. When a woman is pissed off, you have to let her be pissed off. Because nothing you say will take away her fury. Sometimes, a beautiful woman just needs to scream. And you need to let her.

When I reach the living room she is already putting her bra back on and wishing she never came here. I can see it on her face, in her movements, in the way her eyes won't meet mine. In the way her hands hide her breasts like they are something she should be ashamed of. Or like they are some secret now that she needs to keep from me.

"Jenny," I say, and it is barely more than a whisper. It is something you would ask yourself whether it was a cough or a sneeze you just heard on the train because it was almost inaudible but you were sure you heard something.

She buckles her bra in – if that's what they do – and looks at me.

I feel a cold front in her gaze and I think it's too chilly for April. But Hurricane Jenny is standing in my living room with no pants on and I need to make her stop wanting to kill me. I can't afford any more bad karma. And by the look in her eyes, not only has she plotted my death, but she already hired a hitman and got herself an alibi.

"There will be witnesses," I say.

"Witnesses?" she shrieks. "What fucking witnesses?" She is frantic and searching for the rest of her clothes.

I think about Sabrina in the closet and I'm so pissed off

that she can't cover for me because she doesn't have a brain and she isn't real and how do I make this woman stop? "Jenny, please, calm down."

"Calm down?!" she shrieks. "You calm down! Where the fuck are my pants?"

I glaze over the living room and find her pants behind the sofa and go to pick them up but she smacks my hand.

"Don't you touch my pants!" she says.

"Okay," I say, with my hands up like the prisoner she's made me. "I won't touch your pants."

She's pulling them on like her parents just caught us fucking in their bedroom. And she's rattling off curse words and names at me.

I just want to make it better but it's all too confusing. "Jenny, please." And now, for some reason, I want the determined Jenny back. The one who thinks I'm worth fighting for, the one worth stalking via text.

But her clothes are on. And yet again, I'm watching a woman scramble for the door.

"I never meant to hurt you," I say. And it's true. They never believe it though. Probably because we usually don't try hard enough to mean it.

"Fuck you," she says, as she reaches the door.

But I know Jenny well enough to know that she doesn't want to leave. At least like this. Maybe she doesn't want to leave at all.

I softly press against the door to keep her from opening it and wait for her to say something.

"You suck," she says, quietly, without looking at me.

"I know," I say. "I'm sorry. I really never meant to hurt you."

"You guys never do."

"We really don't."

"No," she says. "Not that you don't mean to hurt us. You just never mean it."

"Never mean what?"

"This. All of it. You never mean anything you fucking do. None of you. And you think it doesn't affect us."

I look down because if she's right, that bothers me.

"You guys just love to complain about women. You like to say that we nag you. That we bitch. That we talk and do too much. Well guess what? We do too much to overcompensate for all the shit you guys don't do. We do too much because the majority of you don't do enough."

I am silent.

"We do too much and you do nothing but complain about it. When really, you should fucking appreciate it."

I am still silent. I don't know how to say I appreciate it when I have been ignoring her for days. Because really, I haven't appreciated it. "Jenny..."

"No," she says. "Just let me go."

And then she's moving past me toward the door I'm blocking before I can try to convince her to stop. Because I can't convince her to stop. She is four steps away from never talking to me again and I am one regret away from feeling like I may have just ruined the possibility of a good thing.

Life, sometimes it gives you a rough hand to play with. Sometimes it gives you too good of a hand to even know where to start. All you can do is play until you're out. Until someone beats you. Or you can count your cards and try to fool them all. But usually, you get caught. One way or another.

TEN

IT HAS BEEN three hours since Jenny stormed out in a post-sex ridden rage. I should be better at comforting people. Maybe I should just be better at convincing people. But I can't convince people of something if there are facts that don't need to be presented in the argument.

Fact: Jenny was a one-night stand.

Fact: Jenny is now more than a one-night stand.

When you sleep with someone on more than one occasion, the one-night stand argument goes out the window. But you can't argue with a woman when she has her mind set on something. The bottom line is she feels used, and I can't fault her for that. Maybe I did use her. I didn't mean to. I just wanted the comfort and company she was offering.

I didn't hit on her, she came on to me. So really, she got what she wanted in the end. Which was me. I guess she just didn't get me the way she wanted me. Or maybe she just wanted to be the one to say goodbye this time. If that's what she wanted, she got it.

I've washed my hands four times since she left and I took

another shower. I look at Sabrina who is next to me on the couch. After Jenny's little rant, I felt bad holding Sabrina hostage in the closet. Maybe she can't feel anything, but if she could, I wouldn't want her to feel like I was ashamed of her, or like I was using her, too.

She's just a doll, I remind myself. She doesn't care either way, because she can't care. But still, it feels nice sitting on the couch and not feeling so alone. And Sabrina doesn't storm out on me. She doesn't leave me alone to question my existence and purpose. She doesn't make me feel like a worthless piece of shit. She just...*is*. She is a silicone body plopped down on the couch next to me, willing to ride the wave. She'll watch the game. She'll sit here as I drink and smoke. She won't tell me I smell. Won't tell me I'm drinking too much. Won't push me away and tell me I taste like an ashtray if I try to kiss her. She just is. And she lets me be me.

I made sure the door was locked in case either of my crazies come back to me. But neither of them will. Usually, when a woman decides to leave, she is gone. If she has done the deciding, she is gone, and there's no getting her back. No sense in trying.

When the sun goes to sleep and the moon takes over I decide to go out for a drink. A few blocks away, I can catch a buzz in public. Somewhere where a doll's eyes won't stare at me.

I'm on a barstool ordering another beer before last call when I feel the shoulder brush against me.

"Oh, sorry," she says, with a giggle.

"Don't worry about it," I say, with the most of a smile I can muster up. And I take a swig of my Heineken.

"Can I have three lemon drops?" she asks the bartender.

"Sure thing, beautiful," he says, and he pours them for her.

And he's hoping one is for him. I can see it in his eyes as he looks at her. But she slides one over to me.

"That's just because you're cute and alone," she says. "And because you look sad."

I laugh. "I look sad, do I?" And I take the shot glass and thank her. "Cheers." We clink shot glasses and down the shots. I don't know what the hell was in that but it was gross. Only the smile on her face and the flirty look in her big brown eyes make it worth it.

Her friend drinks hers down and looks at us, questioning, then goes back to dancing.

"I'm Sam," the cute girl says, holding out her hand.

"Alan," I say, shaking it with my own. "Thank you. That was very considerate of you." I look at the bartender. "I'll cover those shots."

He gives me a nod as I slide two twenties over the counter.

"Noooo," she says, dragging it out. "It was my treat!"

"I insist," I say.

"Why?"

I shrug. "I don't know. I just think the man should always pay. Call me old-fashioned."

"Wow, you mean to tell me I've found a real, live gentleman out in the wilderness?" she says, leaning against the bar.

I laugh. She has no idea what kind of "gentleman" I am. But I know what she wants before she even wants me to know, because she is already giving me that look. It's too soon for that look and I figure she must be pretty drunk. I look over at her friend, who is clumsily dancing by herself, with her eyes closed. "Sam, I think you and your friend should head home for the night."

She looks over at her girlfriend and in a slurred voice says, "Oh, she's fiiiine."

"How are you two getting home?" I ask.

"We're walking," she says. Then she looks at her girlfriend and the bartender. "Three more shots, please!"

He looks at me and I shake my head and call him over. "They've had enough."

He nods, then walks off to another customer.

"Hey!" Sam calls after him.

But he's long gone.

"Come on, I'll walk you girls home," I say.

Sam grabs onto my arm for support as she stumbles when she tries to explain to me how they are fine, that they can make it home by themselves. But it's almost 2am and I'm not hearing it.

"Grab your friend. Let's go," I say.

"Jessica!" she says, pulling at the leggy blonde's arm. "Come on. It's time to go."

Her friend reluctantly agrees after she attempts to take a drink from her empty cup. "But the shots?"

"There are no more shots," Sam says. "He's gonna walk us home."

The drunk Jessica takes one look at me and says "Oooooh, is he now?"

I extend both my arms so they can grab on for dear life. And all I can think is that it's going to be a long walk with two drunk girls who don't know whether they're coming or going.

ELEVEN

BY THE TIME we reach the sidewalk, Jessica vomits. Sam runs over to hold her hair back and almost trips over nothing in her heels on the way. I look away, because if I smell or see puke, I will want to puke. I hold my breath and look away.

I haven't breathed in maybe a second too long and I inhale deeply out of instinct. The scent of puke sneaks in and I instantly wish I was still holding my breath. I look at Sam, who is rubbing Jessica's back, with her head turned sideways, probably trying not to throw up herself. Girls are just so comforting. To each other. To us. I can't help but smile a little at the sight of them.

After what seems like an hour, Jessica mumbles an embarrassed "I'm sorry".

But I shake my head and look at the girl with messy bleach blonde hair. "Don't be. Don't ever apologize for puking your guts out at 2am."

She nods her pretty little inebriated head in agreement and I hold my arm out for her to take. She grabs onto it like a lifeboat and steadies herself. "Thanks for being so nice," she says, a pink flush in her cheeks, even though she has nothing to be embarrassed about.

"You shouldn't have to thank any guy for being nice."

Sam grabs onto my other arm and tugs. "Psst," she says.

I look down and over at her. She's smiling. With that look in her eye again that says she wants to rip my clothes off right here.

"Most guys aren't this nice. We appreciate it," she says.

And it breaks my heart for a minute, because they shouldn't be this grateful. This appreciative. "Most guys are fucking assholes," I say. "You shouldn't trust us." And I say "us" because I am one of them, and I extend my hand but I don't remove it from her grip. "Lead the way."

"We're only a few blocks from here," she says. "Come on." And she starts walking.

Jessica is drunk. Too drunk. Her heels aren't cooperating with her and she is too slow. She is slowing me and Sam down, so after another half a block I look at her. "Okay, blondie. Come on." And I bend down a little, but she doesn't take the bait.

"What?" she says, eyes half-closed.

"Hop on," I say, my body still bent.

She figures it out and piggybacks me while Sam laughs.

"I'm jealous," Sam says.

And I only smile in response, but it's not what she hoped I'd respond with, because she's disappointed. I can feel it in the way she loosens her grip on my arm.

"Do you live close to here?" she asks.

"Yeah, not too far."

Jessica is hardly latching on around my neck and I have to hoist her ass up with my right hand and remind her to hold on. She only responds with a garbled sigh and I bend forward a little more to make sure she doesn't fall backwards as my hand grips her thigh.

"Where's your girlfriend tonight?" Sam asks.

And it's always the same. Assuming I have a girlfriend. Assuming I am taken. Assuming this or that. Really, it's just their way of trying to figure out whether or not I am single. Whether or not I could possibly be theirs. "We broke up recently," I say. Because I like the attention of a beautiful woman. Because I know she wants to fuck me. Because I know if I wanted, she could potentially be my next girlfriend. If she wanted to be. But I also know that drunk sex and one-night-stands with strangers often lead to no real relationship. Especially if she doesn't remember the night you met.

"Oh, I'm sorry," she says. But she isn't. Her grip around my arm tightens again, this time with a little squeeze.

"It's okay," I say. "It happens."

We've walked for almost three blocks now and Sam is getting more and more tired. I can tell by the way her heels start dragging. And I look at her feet.

"Don't those hurt?" I ask, eyeing her heels.

She giggles. "Yeah, they're definitely not as comfortable as slippers, but they only really get uncomfortable after you walk enough in them. I mean, some, they can feel like pillows as long as you're not doing laps. Others, they hurt after walking more than three minutes in them. It just depends."

"It always depends, huh?"

"What do you mean?" she asks.

"I don't know. Everything always depends, really. On circumstances," I say. And I regret it. I don't know what I'm trying to say. I am caught up in the chilly breeze and the fact that I have two beautiful young women literally attached to me right now. And I can feel Jessica's tits on my back but that's not what's making me horny. Sam's caressing on my arm is.

"True," she says, sliding her fingers up and down my arm. "And what are your circumstances now?"

I know where this is going. But I don't make it obvious. Because unfortunately, tonight, it is not going there. "I'm just going through something right now. I'm not really, available, even though I am. If you know what I mean."

She nods and her fingers stop gliding, but she doesn't let go. She is persistent. "When do you think you will be available? I'm a pretty patient person."

But, it's after 2am, and she's drunk. "I don't know if you'll even remember my name by tomorrow," I remind her.

"Oh, I will." She lets go of my arm and takes her phone out of her purse. "What's your phone number, Alan? I think we should stay in touch until you become available. Because I'm very available, but I think I could make myself unavailable for you."

She's good, because I smile even though I don't mean to, then I rattle off the random digits that make up my phone number until she's content. And she calls me. *Just so I have hers, too.*

She asks me what her name was. But I don't tell her. Some things are better left unsaid. And sometimes you don't want to have another Alice/Jenny situation, just in case. As we walk, she tells me about her lying, cheating ex. And all I can think is that I'm a lying, cheating ex, too. She just wouldn't want to hear that right now. So I keep walking, letting her think she met a good guy for a change.

We reach the stoop outside her apartment and I let Jessica down gently, asking if Sam needs help getting her up the stairs. Of course she says yes. But that's not why she wants me going upstairs.

I know it's a bad idea as soon as she fidgets with her keys and opens the door. She's nervous. She's planning this out in her head. Right now, she only has one goal.

I carry Jessica up the three flights of stairs and to a door. 4B. Sam opens the door and I smell vanilla or lilacs or something fresh and sweet. Either way, it's nice. And she points to the door where Jessica's room is. So I carry her in there and gently flop her on the bed. Well, as gently as I can, considering how dead weight she is at this point. And snoring. Sam motions for me to close the door. So I do.

She kicks off her shoes and jumps on me. Shit. She kisses me before I can consider whether or not this is a good idea. But she's such a good kisser, all deep and sensual and passionate, and my right hand is holding up her ass while the left is gripping her hair and gently tugging.

She moans into my mouth in response. That's when my dick starts getting hard. Her hands are around my neck, playing with my hair, rubbing it. Gripping my shoulders. Tossing her head back as I kiss her neck.

"You seem pretty available to me," she says, in a raspy desperate voice, as I touch her through her jeans.

"I'm not," I say, as I stop the motion and move my hand. "Look, I just need you to kn.."

"Shhh," she says, covering my mouth with her hand. "Tell me after. Right now, I just need you to fuck me."

And no other words could elicit such a response from me as she pulls her own top off and throws it god knows where. We are hands and kisses and breaths and curses until I feel my phone vibrate in my pocket.

It vibrates again a moment later.

She tries to kiss me deeper, but I'm distracted now. I move to put her down and she's trying to savor the moment.

"No," she whimpers. "Let it go."

But her greatest fear is my biggest hope as I pull my phone out of my pocket and see two text messages from Alice.

"I can't help it," the first text says.

"I miss you."

Sam is disappointed when I tell her that I'm sorry. And she has every right to be. Right now, she only wants one thing from me. One thing that I normally would deliver, but can't. Won't.

"She left you," she says. "I wouldn't."

"You would," I say. "I'm sorry." And I turn my back to head for the door but she stops me.

"Don't fucking sacrifice yourself for women that don't appreciate you. Please," she says.

Those words stop me in my tracks for a moment as I look into her big brown eyes. She is standing in front of me, eyes begging. She is the living, breathing epitome of sorrow and desire and promise. I want to stay. I want to forget Alice. But I can't. No one ever said the heart was smart.

She moves her hands to me and lets them rest upon my shoulders. "I would never let you be available, not like this."

Her words sting. I can't let her know she has affected me but I'm sure my face says it all as I avert my eyes. Anything other than seeing another woman I've let down in some way.

"I'm sorry," I manage.

Two hands gripping my face.

"You have nothing to be sorry for," she says. "Look at me."

I force my eyes to meet hers, trying to ignore the disappointment in them.

"Don't you ever fucking love a woman who doesn't appreciate you, okay?" she says, with a firmness in her voice that surprises even her.

I nod. "Don't you ever fucking love a man who doesn't appreciate you either, okay?"

She lets go and provides a silent agreement with a slight nod. "This could have been something, you know?" she says.

"I know," I say. Then I lean forward and kiss her on the cheek. "Bye, Sam. Don't go getting wasted at bars again just to leave with guys you don't know."

I turn my back and open the door before she can say anything else, because she doesn't know how much her words have meant to me. How much they make me wish I could stay and be the guy she thinks that I am.

TWELVE

SOME WOMEN ARE JUST BORN romantics. All hope and promise and no holding back, even after they've been hurt. Even after they've questioned whether love really exists or if it only exists in their hearts. In their potential for loving the way they want to love and be loved. Like Sam.

As I walk down the stairs, leaving Sam behind, I know I have made my choice between my past/present and possible future. But if anyone were to ask me today, or yesterday, or tomorrow, I would choose Alice again. I will choose Alice every time. Every single time. Because sometimes what a woman does to you changes you. Sometimes it is out of your hands. Sometimes, it *is* her hands.

I'm texting her back as I'm walking down the stairs and finally hit send once I make it outside to the sidewalk.

"I miss you too," I say.

I'm not that far from home so I'm walking, at a steady pace. Knowing that if there's any shot in hell for her to come over this late, I'd need to be home right now if not sooner.

When my phone doesn't buzz I look down at it and check it again.

No text from Alice. It is 2:56am at this point and I wonder if she's just drunk and already regretting what she said in a moment of honesty. Maybe she's sleeping. Maybe she hit send and crawled into bed and shut her phone off. But all I can think as my feet are moving is, *please be awake.*

I'm too sober for this. My heartbeat is erratic and thumping around while I think about every possible mistake I may have made already. Jenny. Sam. The bar. The pier. Witnesses. Holding hands with another woman. Leaving the bar with another woman. Two women, actually. Sleeping with another woman. Almost sleeping with the other, other woman.

The air has a slight chill and I rub my hands together then reach for my pack of cigarettes. I open the pack and slide one out, reaching for my lighter. But when I put the Marlboro menthol in my mouth I take it out and put it back in the pack. Alice wouldn't want me to taste like an ashtray. And this is it. She's coming back to me. Even if it isn't tonight, I know she wants to. That's all I need right now. Not this fucking cigarette. And not a night in another woman's bed. A woman who is not Alice.

I walk three more blocks before I reach my building. In that time, I have checked my phone four times, thinking maybe it vibrated and I missed it. Still no text from Alice. I slip my phone back into my pocket and my key in the door then lock it behind me. I walk upstairs.

There is no vibrating, still. No reassurance left for a loser like me. I open my apartment door with a different key, with the same disappointment. My feet feel heavy now as the hour of the night and the realization hits me. It's 3am. And she isn't going to answer tonight.

The first thing I do is wash my hands. Twice. Then I open the cabinet door in the kitchen and take out the whiskey and pour myself a shot and drink it down. And then another. And another. And another. And one more just to make sure I can just about feel almost nothing for the rest of the night.

It's only when the drink hits that I finally light a cigarette. Accepting my fate for the night. Alice isn't answering. She isn't coming. It's just me in this empty apartment. And I go to my bedroom and look at the closet door. Me, and Sabrina. With a layer of guilt baked into my now inebriated mind, I open the door handle and pull her out. She's heavier at 3am. Not as light. Not as delicate. I can almost hear her say "no" as I lay her body on the bed. Because she isn't in the mood. And neither am I.

But still, I hike up her skirt and I take my dick out and I fuck her. Because I have to. I need to.

And when it's over, I put her back in the closet. The shame isn't new. The guilt isn't either. At this point, neither is the doll. Sabrina is getting old, just like me. What a fucking pair we make, I think, as I go into the kitchen and pour myself three more shots.

The daylight hits me like a god damn brick. I fell asleep wearing my clothes and I pull out my sweatshirt just enough to sniff it. Maybe I'm insane, but I think I can still smell Sam on it. Her perfume. Her scent. The aroma that was *her*. I look for my phone like a lunatic, tossing the bed covers around. Looking on my nightstand. The dresser. The floor.

I find it in the kitchen. On the counter next to the empty shot glass and the whiskey. It's dead. I charge it. I wash my hands. I sit on the couch next to where my phone is plugged in and when it turns on, I look at it. The zero new texts fucking thing isn't a mirage. And I know I'm fucked if Alice tried to call me. If it went straight to voicemail she would think I was ignoring her. Or that I was with someone else. Or out somewhere. And now I'll never know. I want to bash my head against the wall. I want to know if she tried to call. I want to know if she still misses me now that the sun came up.

I'm frustrated. And I fucking miss her. And now I'm getting angry just thinking about it. So I do the only thing I can do. I masturbate. In fury. Thinking about all this mixed in with sexual memories of Alice. And when I finish, it's violent, but it's calming. People who don't need sex the way I do will never understand what it's like. Needing it. Needing the release. And then hating yourself for it right after.

I go take a hot shower and brush my teeth. Then, I make two cups of coffee. One, for me. One, for Alice, in case she shows up.

Even though I know she won't.

PART TWO

THEN

THIRTEEN

I AM NINE YEARS OLD. My father is passed out from the drink already and it's not even dark yet. His friend from work is in the kitchen, talking to my mother. I am in the doorway, watching. Listening. Someone has to watch out for her when Dad gets like this.

"You make a mean meatloaf, Mrs. Shaden," he says.

"Thanks, Fred. Help yourself. I have to run to the store," she says. She wipes her hands on her apron and then takes it off and hangs it up. She notices me in the doorway. "Alan, honey," she says, as she bends down and rubs my hair. "Mommy has to run to the store real quick. You be nice to Mr. Smith, okay?" And she kisses me on the cheek.

I nod. And by store, she means the liquor store. But we both know that and we both know that neither of us has to say it out loud. She is probably almost at the point where she's ready to pass out too, but she likes to start drinking later. Within three hours, she'll be passed out on the couch, unless Dad wakes up and drags her into the bedroom to do that thing to her that makes her cry out. Sometimes it's in a good way, I guess. But sometimes it isn't. It all sounds bad to me.

When the front door shuts behind her, I stay where I am. Looking at my father's friend. His co-worker. His pal. I wonder what my mother sees in him. Why she lets him stay for dinner when he drives my father home from work.

He pops open another Bud Light and drinks the whole thing down in one or two gulps. Then he burps and looks at me. "Hey, kid. You having fun tonight yet?"

I'm not, but I nod anyway. Mom always told me to be polite to grown-ups and Dad always told me to respect his god damn friends.

"Wanna have some more fun?" he says.

I don't move as he stumbles toward me. "Like what?" I ask.

He takes two nervous looks around and grabs me by the arm. "Come on, kid. I'll show you what fun is. Let's play a game."

I am no match for his strength. My nine-year-old body is an ant compared to this giant of a man and I wonder what he wants to do. "I have a Nintendo," I say, full of innocence and seriousness and confusion.

"To hell with Nintendo, kid," he says. And he looks at me and puts his finger over his mouth to tell me to stay quiet.

I nod. And now I wonder what he wants to do. Part of me is curious. Part of me is afraid. Part of me is excited. Maybe he'll sneak me out and we'll go throw toilet paper over the neighbors' trees or something. Maybe we'll go outside and explore the woods, looking for monsters or werewolves now that it's dark. Maybe we'll leave this house and he'll take me to a different one. A better one.

But he leads me down the basement stairs and when he

doesn't turn the lights on, I know something isn't right but maybe something isn't exactly wrong either.

"What are you..." I squeak out. But his hand goes over my mouth.

"You ever done anything with other kids?" he asks, in a hoarse whisper.

"Like what?" I ask. "I play games with them sometimes and..."

"Yeah, games," he says, and his tone is just above a whisper now. "This is like a game. Only it feels good."

"For who?" I ask.

He laughs. "Shit, kid. It's fun for everyone who's brave enough to play."

"Maybe we should go back upstairs. My mom will be home soon and..."

"You are brave, aintcha?" he asks.

"Of course I am," I say. Because I am. I am brave. I have to be. Always. Mom and Dad always tell me I have to be.

"Then here," he says.

But it's dark. I can't see. Then I feel his hands find mine.

"You know that little thing between your legs, kid?" he asks. He doesn't wait for a response. "I don't know if you've touched it yet, but it feels good when you do. Like this. I'll show you."

Even in the dark I can see him kneel in front of me. I can hear the unzip of his pants. I turn away, feeling like I'm invading something. Like it's something he should do in private. But he puts something in my hand and without looking I know what it is. And he tells me what to do. And he says he is showing me, for my own good. So I know how to do it by myself later on.

He tells me this is what boys do. And sometimes they do

it together. When he asks if my dad showed me yet, I tell him no.

"Never has been that good of a dad, huh?" he says.

"No," I say, moving my small hands like he says to.

"Well, don't ever tell him about this. He'd probably be sad that you learned it from someone else when it was his job to show you. And it would make your mom sad, too. And your parents are sad enough, ain't they?"

I nod, but he can't see me. And I sit there, in the dark, with this foreign object in my hands, thinking my dad could have showed me this, so I didn't have to learn from some stranger in a basement. He could have been brave enough to show me himself.

And when Fred says I need to put it in my mouth to see if I like it, because it's the only way to know whether or not I like boys, I do. Because I am brave. Because he says it's the only way to know for sure.

And by the time my mom gets home, I know, for sure, I definitely do not like boys.

FOURTEEN

I AM WASHING my hands after dinner. I am eleven years old. Fred still comes by after work, after he drops my dad off. Sometimes, when Mom goes to the store, he takes me into the basement. Like tonight. But I told him I don't like boys. I told him I don't want to put his thing in my mouth.

He says he could do it to me. I say no. It doesn't seem right. But he pushes.

"You could see if you like it," he says. "Just, to see how it feels."

"I don't think I want to," I say.

"Hey, little man, it will feel good," he says. "Watch."

And I push him away when he reaches for me. "No," I say.

"You don't want to feel good?" he asks, as he takes a chug of his beer. "Fine. Then you can do it for me."

I hear the unzip of his pants and remember how bad it felt. "Fine," I say. "Fine."

"That'a boy," he says. "Here, to help make it easier."

He hands me his beer and I take my first sip. It tastes disgusting. I cough it up.

"It gets easier," he says. "Just like this will. Lay down."

Mom is at the store and Dad is passed out on the couch. And I know it's either him doing this to me, or me doing it to him. So I grab the beer and drink it down as fast as possible. By the time I lay down, my head feels different. And when his hand is on me, it doesn't feel good, but it doesn't feel bad either.

"I know you don't like boys," he says. "So close your eyes and pretend I'm a girl."

So I do. And it feels good but I'm not sure how, because it also feels terrible.

When it's over, he wipes his mouth with his arm and chugs his beer. "You sure you don't like boys? Sure seems like you do."

And in that moment, I'm not so sure anymore.

FIFTEEN

MOM SAYS she's going to the store. Fred is over. He looks at me. I look at my mom. I want her to stay. I am almost thirteen years old now.

"Can I come with you, Mom?" I ask.

"No, honey, it's late. Why don't you go get in bed, okay?" she says, without giving me a kiss. "I gotta hurry up. They close in fifteen minutes."

Fred is leaning against the counter, drinking his beer. His belly has gotten bigger since I saw him last. He was muscle, big, strong. Now, he's just big and kind of fat. When the door closes behind her, he crushes the can and throws it in the recyclables bin.

"Come on, kid. How bout we try a new game?" he says.

Before I can say no, he's got me by the arm. Taking me to the basement.

Tonight feels different. He's had more to drink than usual. And usually he drinks a lot. Tonight, it's a lot more than a lot. He can hardly walk straight as he finds the doorknob to the basement.

"Come on, we gotta be quick," he says.

I want to yell for my dad, but he doesn't care enough anyway. To stop Fred. To tell me or show me himself. What my boy parts do. How they're supposed to feel. What you're supposed to do with them.

Fred leaves the lights off as usual. And when we get to the bottom of the stairs, he hands me a beer he brought. "Here, kid," he says. "Soon, you won't be a kid anymore."

"What do you mean?" I ask, opening the can and taking a sip. "I thought I already wasn't a kid anymore."

"Drink up, little man," he says. And he hands me something small. "Drink it. All of it."

It burns as it goes down. It is not like the beer. It is stronger. Almost instantly, it makes me feel different. I choke on some of it as it goes down, burning my lungs.

"Quiet, kid," he says. "Drink the rest of it. You're gonna need it."

I know better by now than to ask questions I don't want the answers to. So I don't ask why. I stay quiet and drink it. My head is swimming and I feel like I am not here. But that's okay. Because I don't want to be here. Fred knows it. I know it.

"You're a big boy now," he says, breaking the silence.

"What do you mean?" I ask.

"There's one more test. To see if you like boys or girls," he says.

"But I already told you, I like girls. I definitely like girls. Only girls."

"But last time, you liked it. And I'm a boy," he argues. "How can you be sure?"

"I'm sure. I know I'm sure," I say.

"Ehh, I don't know about that, kid. Seems pretty gay, if you ask me. There's only one way to be certain."

"How?" I ask, confused.

"Take your pants off. If you like it, then you know that you definitely like boys. If you don't, you like girls."

"But I like girls," I say.

"This is the only way you'll know for sure, kid," he says, pulling down his jeans. "Do you want to spend your whole life wondering if you like boys, too? Your daddy should have taught you this by now. You're too old to guess."

He doesn't wait for a response and I don't give him one. Because he's right, my dad should have taught me this by now.

I am buzzed and feeling warm when he touches me. Then he bends over and tells me where to put it, what to do.

It seems disgusting and I tell him so. But he tells me to shut up and just do it before he does it to me. I think that would be the only thing worse, him doing it to me. Having this the other way around.

It feels, okay I guess, but I hate it and I am disgusted and I am ashamed the whole time. I don't want to do it. I don't want to do it ever again. And I hate Fred for making me. I wish it was a girl, any girl, and I wish both of us wanted to.

And when he says it's my turn, I decide this is where even I know this isn't a test or game anymore. I look him in his eyes in the dark and I tell him no. And then I tell him I like girls. *Only* girls. And I tell him I don't want any more tests.

SIXTEEN

I AM thirteen and I'm taller than most of the kids in my grade. My mom doesn't make my lunch but if she does it's just cold leftovers from last night's dinner thrown together in a container, which I don't mind. I prefer cold chicken to nothing. I prefer cold mashed potatoes to stealing muffins and anything else I can get my hands on.

I've been caught six times now, stealing food from the cafeteria. The first time I got a warning. The second and third time, detention. The other kids at school make fun of me for being poor. We are poor, but that's the least of my worries. When I was suspended, my parents gave me shit. Especially my dad. He called me an ungrateful little shit and whipped me with a belt until I couldn't even remember what it felt like to stand up straight or walk. Mom kept her mouth shut. Just what he taught her to do. Although, I do think I heard her cry during it. Every time the belt landed another blow, I think I heard her sobbing get a little louder.

He was drunk. As usual. She probably was too, just not as much. Plus she never became an angry drunk like him. With him it was a really thin line between just enough and too much. Before he would take that last sip to cross him over, he would be calm. Almost happy. Relaxed. But once he had that drink to put him over the edge, he was gone. Different. Mad. Angry. You couldn't say a fucking word to him without him losing his temper for no reason.

So when I'd give him a reason, I think it just made his life easier. At least he had an excuse to beat the shit out of me. At least he wasn't taking it out on my mom. I would look at her, pleading for her to just stay quiet. Because now, I'm getting bigger. She knows it. He knows it. It will only be a matter of time before I put on some weight. Before I'm able to beat the shit out of him, for once. See how he likes it.

There seems to be nothing but time for me. Time, alone. While my mom is working. While my dad is passed out. While I hide in my room from both of them. All I can do is sit here and masturbate. Because I'm angry and bored. And feelings surge in my body that I didn't ask for. And I hate that every time I do it, every time I jerk off, afterward I'm reminded of Fred. Because he's the one who showed me how to do it. He's the one who touched me for the first time. The first one I touched. It makes me feel disgusting. And gross. And gay. Just like he said.

I know I'm not gay, but if you get off when another guy jerks you off, does it make you gay? Does it make me gay? The other things he did to me? The other things he had me do to him? He said it sure seemed like I liked it. And that it was pretty gay. I wonder if I am, sometimes. I wonder if he was right. I know I can't tell anyone. They would call me a faggot. They would say I was gay. That I wanted it. That I did it, so I must be. But they don't know that when I jerk off I think of Maggie and her blonde hair and blue eyes. Her soft, full lips. And I picture them around my penis. And I picture her hands touching me instead of my own. And I close my eyes and imagine her, telling me to take my pants off. Telling me that if I finish, I must like it. That if I finish, I must be straight. That it seems like I'm pretty straight when I do. And I close my eyes and imagine it's her cute ass I see through her jeans that I'm entering. That it's her, moaning. And enjoying it. I get up and wash my hands. I shouldn't think of her like that. I would never force her to do that.

I get back into my room and I look at the calendar in my room with x's marked off on the days of this month that have already passed. I am counting down the days. Experiencing this weird puberty thing as I grow. As I harden. It's weird how fast I shot up. Almost like it happened overnight. I got a little chubby and then grew. Thinned out. My penis is growing, too. Just overnight almost it went from being this small thing that was just there to being this bigger thing that is all I can think about. The only thing of mine I know I can protect. And I know it won't end here. This is only the beginning.

I got a little chubby again, then grew again. Thinned out again. I'm still growing. My teachers notice. Some of my friends' moms notice. Some of the girls at school notice. And sometimes I wonder if my dad notices. Sometimes I wonder if he's scared.

He should be.

SEVENTEEN

MY MOM IS in the kitchen, washing dishes. Her glass with vodka and orange juice is on the counter. Half empty. I am fourteen years old.

The radio is playing and she's listening to classic rock. Moving her hips a little as she hums the tune.

I'm watching from the doorway. Because she never likes when I get too close. I am always too close and never far enough away. I'm pretty sure she never wanted me. Never wanted any kids. And I don't know what she hates more. Her life, my dad, or me. Maybe all three, in equal measures. "Want some help?" I ask, even though I know she'll say no.

She must be feeling pretty buzzed by now, because she turns and smiles and says "Sure, honey. Come here."

She never talks to me. Other than pleasantries. Other than "Go to school" and "Get to bed" and "Why are you in here right now? Go to your room. Don't be nosy." She's a lot sweeter than my father. At least she acknowledges me when I walk into a room. For the most part. Even if she is only telling me to get lost.

"You want to wash or dry?" she asks, drying her hands on her apron, before she takes a sip of her vodka orange juice. Then she lights a cigarette and looks at the clock. It is 10:38pm.

"Either is fine," I say, even though I know I'll be doing both, as I take her spot at the sink. I grab the sponge and start scrubbing, letting warm water run over the dirty dishes.

She takes a drag of her cigarette as she leans against the counter and looks at me. *Really* looks at me. "When the hell did you get so tall?" she asks, with a trace of shock in her raspy tone.

And she's right. By now, I'm taller than she is. Her petite frame, about five inches shorter than me already. My shoulders, much broader than hers. I don't know what to say, but I feel my cheeks get hot. My mom never looks at me. "I don't know," I say. "I guess it just happened."

"I guess the hell it did!" she says, and now, there's amusement in her tone. "My god, Alan Shaden, are you taller than your father?"

I shrug even though I want to say "Not yet, Mom. Not yet."

She sighs and flicks her cigarette ash into the ashtray next to her glass, that is now almost completely empty. "You know, you're awfully quiet. Always have been."

"Me?" I ask, unsure what she means. Even though I want to tell her all she does is tell me to be quiet or go away. She never wants me to speak. Her or Dad.

"Yeah, you," she says.

"You never ask me anything," I say, looking at the dishes as I scrub a ketchup stain off a plate.

"You don't ever seem like you wanna be asked," she says.

Without looking at her, I say "I do."

"Well, in that case, what's your favorite color?" she asks, her smile cracking like the sky just opened up.

I can't help but laugh so I do.

"Ahhh, your little dimples, Al!" she says, pinching my cheeks. "When did my little boy become so damn handsome?" she says, nudging me in the ribs.

I try to stop smiling so she can't talk about my dimples or my smile anymore. "Blue," I say.

"Huh?" she asks, putting out her cigarette and finishing her drink.

"Blue. Blue is my favorite color," I say. And I don't even recognize my own voice when I speak to her. It changes around her. It becomes softer. Shy. And I wonder what it would be like if she hugged me for once. If she hates that color. If she hates me.

She nods. "Okay. Blue it is," she says, walking to the fridge. She makes herself another drink. Then she slinks down the hallway into their bedroom without saying goodnight.

Thirty minutes later, I hear her start to sob.

EIGHTEEN

IT IS CHRISTMAS EVE, I am fifteen years old. I am in my room, just finished washing my hands after jerking off. I'm playing music to drown out the sounds of my father raping my mom. It's snowing in New Jersey. Soft white snowflakes sprinkle the earth and remind me that it is never too late to fall. Even if people have plans. Even if it's not supposed to start snowing until the morning. Even if you want to just get up and go somewhere.

Maggie gave me a Christmas card and a kiss on the cheek. I think she noticed my boner through my pants when she hugged me. Because she leaned into it and pressed herself against it. And then after school, she waited for me outside. Just to tell me she hopes I like her card. But Maggie, she has no idea how much I like her card. How much I like her.

I think of the snow falling around her pale face and blue eyes when I jerk off. I think of her telling me she loves me. Her touching me. And somehow, when I finish, I always wind up back to thinking of Fred. So I get up and wash my hands and remind myself that Fred didn't do that. Maggie did. Maggie did.

I wash my hands again. It never goes away. By the time I get into bed, my mother's crying has stopped. I don't even hear soft snores as I fall asleep with my headphones on.

I wake up to the scent of bacon and eggs. Mom is cooking breakfast. And I wait in my room until she yells for me. Because I can't get up to go take a piss too early. I can't wake them up. I can never wake them up. I have to wait to speak until I am spoken to.

But when she calls for me, I'm already dressed in a new pair of shorts and a sweatshirt. By now, most of my pants don't fit. They're all too short. I'm growing faster than I thought I would. My dad still hasn't noticed. If he did, he never mentioned it. I go into the kitchen and find them already sitting at the table. My dad, wearing a stern face. He isn't happy in the mornings. He won't let himself drink until noon. My mom, on the other hand, is smiling, urging me to eat my bacon. To drink my milk. To finish the eggs and toast.

"Hurry up!" she says. "We don't have all day." Then she smiles. Her smiles are so rare.

I fight back a grin and start to eat. Maybe she got me some new pants. Maybe she has a cab outside waiting to take me to who the fuck knows where. Maybe the time has finally come for them to tell me I'm adopted or something. But when I finish my breakfast, I go to put my plate in the sink and she slaps my hand down.

"To hell with that!" she says. "Get in here!" Then she grabs my wrist and pulls me from the table.

When we get into the living room, I notice. There is blue garland all around it. Blue ornaments on the Christmas tree. Blue wrapping paper on a small pile of presents. Blue Christmas lights on the tree.

I feel something inside I've never felt before until now. Something that feels almost like love. Something that feels like happiness.

My father finishes his breakfast and comes to stand in the doorway of the living room. "What's with all the fucking blue?" he asks.

"You should know," my mother says.

And for a moment, I'm afraid. But as I stand next to my mother, eight inches shorter than me, with my father beside me, now three inches shorter than me, I realize she's right. He *should* fucking know. And it hits me. The day has come. I'm bigger than him now. And I turn to look at him. My voice is deeper now. My body, redefined.

"Yeah," I say. "You should fucking know."

And he puffs his chest out like he is going to have a rebuttal. And it seems like his first instinct is to swing. Until his eyes raise to look at me. Until he finally looks at me. Sees me. For the first time in years. Maybe for the first time in his entire life. In my entire life. And he shrinks back down. "I'm going to get a beer. All this blue is giving me a god damn headache," he says, and he turns to head back into the kitchen.

And I throw my arm over my mother's shoulder. Because for the first time, she chose me.

NINETEEN

I AM sixteen years old and taller than my father before he realizes I am here and he can no longer control me. I get home from school and wipe my bloody mouth, still reeling from the fight I got into earlier.

I walk into the house after school and go to my room to do my homework. It's one of the only things I can do. One of the only things that will make me graduate and get out of this house. My mom is still at work when he gets home.

Fred brings him home but he won't come in the house anymore. Not since the last time he saw how big I got, how much bigger I am than he is now. I know he remembers. Because I do, too.

My dad walks into the kitchen and cracks open a beer. I can hear the faint sizzle and pop. The familiar sound of a can opening. We've learned to ignore each other. Usually he pretends I'm not here and I pretend he isn't here either.

But not today. I hear his footsteps creep down the hallway and stop just outside my door. Then the knock comes.

"It's open," I say, tone void of emotion but maybe not surprise.

"Hey, son," he says.

I look up at him from my notebooks. From my bed too small for my size. "Hey." I refuse to call him "Dad" because he isn't one.

"What happened to your lip?" he asks, walking a few steps into the room like he wants a better look.

"I got into a fight at school," I say, without looking up at him.

"Over what?"

Over being called gay. But you wouldn't understand that. "Nothing."

"Did you beat his ass?" my dad asks.

It's only then that I look up at him. "Yeah. I smashed his head into a table."

"Good," he says. "Don't ever let anyone try to hit you."

And I'm wondering if now is the right time to say, like you hit me all these years? Don't ever let anyone do it to me, again? Is that what you mean? But I just nod.

"Your school called me. You're suspended for three days," he says. "But I'm proud of you, boy."

"Proud of me for what?" I ask.

"For not taking any shit," he says. Then he turns and closes the door behind him before I can say a word.

My mother gets home a few hours later. She is tired from her job, but still, she cooks us dinner. Chicken cutlets and mashed potatoes and green beans. She calls me and my father from our rooms to come eat.

My dad is already drunk. Mom is on her way, but she

only just got started. I'm spent from a long day of school and fighting and pretending. All the pretending is tiring.

The clinks of forks and knives mix together between chewing and gulps of milk. Finally, my mother speaks.

"I heard what happened at school today, Al. Why'd you get into a fight?" she asks.

"He hit me first," I say.

"I just hope you finished it," my father says.

"That's enough, Brent," my mother says. "Don't teach him that."

"Why the hell not? If someone starts it, he better finish it," he says.

She slams her fork down and looks at me without paying him any attention. "God damn it," she says, her voice elevated, which is unusual for her. "Don't you ever be like your father."

"What the hell is that supposed to mean?" he asks, though it is barely a question.

"You know what it means," she says. "Just what I fucking said."

"Get in the room," he says, without even standing up.

And I know he's talking to her, not me.

She gets up from her spot at the table and slams the chair in, pushing it under the table. Then she knocks over his glass of milk with her hand so it spills on his lap. Out of pure spite. We all know it.

She hasn't made it six full steps before my father is out of his chair, grabbing her by the hair. One hard backhand across her face is all it takes for me to jump up, too. Normally, they don't do this in front of me.

My body is moving before I am. He throws his chair at her and she dodges it. But I yank him up by the back of his shirt and pin him against the wall then grab his collar and pull him up to meet my eyes.

"If you ever fucking lay a hand on her again, I'll kill you. Do you hear me?" I'm yelling the words in his face. Fear and anger are one hell of a combination, but my hands are steady, my voice firm.

His glossy dark eyes are looking back at me for one of the first times. Full of something. Hate. Disgust. Regret. *Fear.*

"You proud of me for not taking any shit now, *Dad?*" I ask, even though it isn't a question. "How bout I finish it this time? Because you're fucking done. Do you hear me? Done."

He looks at me with a hardened expression like he's going to do something. But he only squints and swallows back all the shit he wants to say, wants to do.

"Alan, let him go!" my mom cries. "Please, stop. Both of you. Just please, stop." She starts to cry and runs over, grabbing me off him. "Please, don't hurt him. Don't hurt him."

I release him and let him go. Now, it's my mother trying to hug my father. Trying to cradle him. He pushes her away.

"Please, don't hurt him," she wails. Her hands are over her eyes now. "Just please don't hurt him. My baby. My baby. My baby." She's on the floor. Rocking. And crying. And rocking. "Please, don't hurt my baby," she's whispering.

And in that moment, I don't know if she means me or him. I don't know which baby she wants to protect. Or who her baby is. But as my father grabs his beer and chugs it, and gives me one last cold stare, we both know what just happened. I stepped up to him for the first time. And he backed down. He lost.

He doesn't say a word as he opens the kitchen cabinet and pours himself three shots of whiskey. He drinks them, one after another. Then, he lights a cigarette. And pours himself three more. He brings them to the kitchen table and sits in his chair, quietly finishing his dinner at the empty table. Taking a shot in between bites.

His eyes are empty. Staring. The calm is eerie. I wait for him to get up and go ballistic. To start swinging on me. But he doesn't. He eats. And drinks. And smokes. And it's a repetitive cycle until I can no longer stand the sight of him.

I stand in the living room, watching him. His eyes won't meet mine. And I wonder what happened to him to turn a man so cold. So cruel. So fucking heartless.

My mother is still rocking. Still crying. "My baby. My baby."

I can't stand her sobs. I hate when she cries. I just want her to stop. I want to fix it. I want to turn the knobs to adjust our lives to try to make them somewhat normal. I try to help her up but she pushes me away. Eventually, I go into my bedroom to try to sleep, knowing he won't dare try to hurt her anymore, at least for tonight.

Tonight is when I feel it. The shift. The change in the atmosphere, the energy. I am suspended for fighting in school but I will never be suspended for what happens at home because we don't talk about what happens at home. Ever. With each other. Or with anyone. What happens inside these walls stays in here and we all know it. Whether it's for better or for worse. All those times I dialed 911, I never hit send. All those nights I spent listening to my mother cry, I never brought it up. But tonight, in that kitchen, everything changed. I know it. My dad knows it. My mom knows it. And I don't think any of us know what to do from this point forward.

The worst part is knowing that I might be the only one who remembers it tomorrow. Maybe nothing will change. Maybe everything will change. The guessing, the what ifs. The maybe that blackout wasn't really a blackout. Maybe they'll remember it in the morning. Maybe they won't. But I sure as fuck will.

And when I go into my room, and close the door, I change. Then I jerk off. And I hate that I still remember what Fred said.

You wan't to feel good, don't you?

TWENTY

I WAKE up the next morning. I look at the calendar. It is April 4th, 2001 and there is a strange stillness in the house. I look at my alarm. 6:17am. I get up to the sound of silence. Not a single TV is on, not a sound is heard. All there is, is the scent of bacon pouring from the kitchen.

I jerk off to get rid of my morning wood and then I leave my room and wash my hands in the bathroom. When I enter the kitchen, my mother has set the table. But there are only two plates this morning. She doesn't say a word. And I see her glass of vodka and orange juice on the counter. It's only 1/3 full. She's smoking a cigarette and her hands are shaking.

"Mom?" I say.

"Yeah," she says. But her voice is empty. Dead. She's staring at nothing in front of her as I watch her from the entryway.

I make my way to the table and pull out the chair then sit and start to eat because I know that will make her happy. Dad should still be home. We both know it. And we both know he isn't here. So I don't ask her where his plate is.

Because he would be so pissed if he didn't have a plate set for him before work.

She lifts the glass to her mouth and chugs it down then takes one last drag of her cigarette before she puts it out in the overflowing ashtray. She pulls out her chair and sits down. But she doesn't touch her food. She sits there, looking at her plate. Staring.

"Mom..."

"Don't ask," she says. "I don't want to talk about it. Just eat your breakfast."

So I do. I lift the piece of bacon to my mouth. It's burnt to a crisp but it still tastes good, beyond the bitterness of my surroundings. Beyond the emptiness of the table. Beyond the hurt that has gone on too long. Everything around me is numb and I can almost taste it as I chew the bacon repeatedly, forcing it to go down.

I clear my plate in a futile attempt to make her even the slightest bit happy. It doesn't work. Her food is mostly untouched as she clears the dishes and scrapes her food into the garbage.

She doesn't say another word in the entire half hour we sit there. So I excuse myself and go to my room.

An hour later, she leaves for work.

Later that night, she comes home. It is past midnight now and I hear things breaking in the kitchen. I usually leave her alone when she gets like this. So she can scream it out. Break everything in her path that she deems necessary. Normally it doesn't last that long. But tonight, it continues longer than usual. I hear her cry out. Obscenities follow. It's a different cry. A hurt cry. A pain cry. She accidentally hurt herself physically this time in the process. I go into the kitchen.

She's standing at the kitchen sink, where I find her most nights I'm brave enough to face her like this. She's got a towel wrapped around her hand. There are broken plates and dishes on the floor. Glass. Frustrated tears are spilling from her eyes.

I rush over. "Jesus Christ, Mom. Let me see." I gently take her hand and unwrap the towel. It's a small gash but it's bleeding profusely. I wrap the towel around it and apply pressure. "Hold it just like this. Let me go get something to clean this up with."

I go into the bathroom where I find gauze and peroxide and antibiotic ointment. This isn't the first time and I'm sure it won't be the last. I grab a fresh washcloth and take it all with me back into the kitchen. "Here, sit down."

She nods. She's gone. I'm used to seeing her wasted but not this wasted. Her eyes aren't focusing. She's not there. She's fragile. Confused. Disoriented. Words slurring when she does speak. She's mumbling something I can't understand as I wipe away the blood then put peroxide on the gash followed by the antibiotic ointment. I'm wrapping her hand in gauze.

"My baby would be almost 14 by now," she says, and I'm not sure I heard that right.

"What are you talking about?"

She slams her fist on the table. "Your baby sister, Alan. You had a sister. You were supposed to have a sister."

I still my hands and look at her. "What?"

"Her name would have been Alyssa Rose. My poor baby," she says. And the sobs start again. She's weeping into her hands. "My poor baby. My poor baby."

I don't know what to do so I touch her arm, trying to comfort her.

"He did it. He did it. He'll never admit it but he did it."

Her voice gets louder. "He fucking did this! All of this! It's his fault!" The sobbing. "Oh my god. It's my fault. I never got to meet her. I just wanted to hold her. To love her. Now I can't love anyone. Not even you. My own son."

I try to hug her but she pushes me away from her.

"Please," she says. "I just need to be alone."

I leave her, there, in the kitchen. She's crying and rocking. Crying and rocking. Saying the same thing over and over and over again. "I love you, Alyssa Rose. Now, then, and always. Now, then, and always."

I can't take the sounds of her heart breaking on the kitchen floor any longer. I walk away to the sounds of her repeated words echoing off the walls.

"Now, then, and always. Now, then, and..."

She never says a word about him leaving. And I never ask. We both know why he left. And maybe she knows where he went, but she never tells me.

After that, it's all a blur of empty bottles and empty cigarette packs and the sounds of her sobbing. And the fact that I should have a sister. I don't know if she remembers that she told me. I never bring it up again. And neither does she.

TWENTY-ONE

I SILENTLY THANK god for technology as Maggie messages me asking what I'm doing. Asking if I'm still suspended. I tell her yes. I tell her it's been a long day. She wants to come over. Says she misses me and can't stop thinking about me.

I tell her to come over.

An hour later she is knocking on the door and I open it. Her blonde hair is combed back perfectly, looking messy but in a way that tells me she cares but she doesn't. She lets herself in as I open the door and she starts talking about school and who did what today. But I don't care about that. I only care about her and what she did today.

"How was your day?" she asks.

"It was good," I say. "Nothing crazy."

"That's good," she says. "So, where's your room?"

"You want to see it?" I ask, a little embarrassed. I know there are dirty clothes piled up in the corner. My bed is only half-made, and it's only that way because I knew she was coming over. I cleaned as best as I could, but, I'm not the cleanest.

She giggles and blushes. "Of course I do."

I just grin, on accident. Maggie is in my house. Her boobs are popping out of her shirt. Her jeans are tight. She put on makeup. I think something is about to happen. I think she wants something to happen.

I am still a virgin when we enter my bedroom. But I am not one when we exit an hour later. She says I was her first. I tell her she was mine.

She seems unsure afterward, but happy. I feel, like a whole new person. Maggie Grant lost her virginity to me. I lost mine to Maggie Grant. *The* Maggie Grant. I ask her to be my girlfriend and she says yes. And when I let her out a half hour later, I am still trying not to smile. And I watch her blonde hair sway behind her as she leaves. And I look at her ass as she walks away.

I savor her scent on my sheets and pillows for the rest of the day before my mom gets home. And I know, for sure, that I am definitely *not* gay.

And I also know, that Maggie chose *me*. And for the first time, I don't feel ashamed about that.

TWENTY-TWO

MAGGIE and I have been together six months. I wake up, happy. Happy that I have her. Happy that she's mine.

But I am turning off my alarm as I get out of bed. I need to check on my mom. I go into the living room – she doesn't sleep in the bedroom anymore, it's empty – and she is knocked out cold. Still sleeping. She should be up and getting ready for work now, but she hasn't been doing much of that lately.

She drinks, from the moment she wakes up to the moment she passes out. I've started putting water in her vodka so she doesn't kill herself. I check the cabinets to make sure there aren't any pills for her to overdose on. She mentioned killing herself once and I didn't know if I should believe her but it's the kind of thing you don't take risks with. And I started to believe it when I heard her sobbing at 3am. I found her on the bathroom floor, with small yellow pills spread all around her like some sort of halo from hell.

She doesn't want to live anymore. She misses my dad and

I'm pretty sure she hates me because he left. I think if she could have chosen again, she would have chosen him.

I do the same thing I do every morning. I shake her awake, as gently as I can at first. But this time she doesn't respond. "Mom!" I say. She doesn't move but I see her chest rise and fall, in the slightest way. I rush to the phone in the kitchen and call 911. And for the first time, I hit send.

An ambulance arrives ten minutes later. They say it's an overdose. They pump her stomach. Put needles in her arms. Fluids. IV's. Hook her up to machines and stick her in a bed in the emergency room.

Her sister comes about three hours later. My mom is still sleeping. I haven't seen my aunt in almost two years.

She walks in like she just walked off a movie set. "Alan, baby," she says. And she's hugging me, tight. "I'm so sorry. We're gonna make sure she's okay, okay?"

I nod. "Yeah. They said she'll be fine. She just had too much last..."

"She's been having too much for too long," Aunt Angel says. She goes over to the bed and grabs her sister's hand, my mother's hand. "Dee," she says. "Dee, I'm so fucking sorry. I'm gonna make it better, okay? I promise. I'm gonna make it better."

A few hours later, Aunt Angel brings me home and we are in the living room, cleaning up empty glasses and bottles.

"Go pack your things, baby," she says.

"Pack? For what?" I ask.

"You two are coming with me. Your mom is gonna lose the house, anyway. It went into foreclosure."

"What? But we live here. I go to school here. I have a..."

"You'll be coming to live with me," she says. "Go pack your stuff. I'll take care of the rest of the house."

"I have a girlfriend here," I say. "I love her."

"And I'm sure she loves you. But baby, you're young. There'll be plenty more girls later. Go pack your stuff, okay?"

I look at her, into her brown eyes full of conviction and insistence. There won't be other girls like Maggie. I know it. "I want to stay."

"Stay where? This house isn't yours anymore. It's no one's. It belongs to the bank now. Please, I know it's hard, but I'm trying to help. Just pack your stuff, okay?"

I want to scream no. I want to say it isn't okay. None of this shit is okay. But I relent. I accept the stack of boxes she hands to me and I go into my room and start emptying my dresser drawers. I empty my closet. I add my few things into the boxes. And I wait for school to get out so I can talk to Maggie.

When she calls the house, asking where I've been, I tell her to call me. I don't want her to see all this. But she comes over.

She walks into my room as I'm packing one of the last boxes.

"Alan?" she says, her voice small and quiet and questioning.

I drop my box and go to her. I lift her up into a hug.

"What's going on?" she asks. "What the hell is..."

"I have to go, Maggie. I'm moving. My mom, she's not doing that great. I'll be staying with my aunt for a little while but I want to be with..."

"Were you even gonna tell me?" she asks, tears burning her eyes.

"Of course I was." I say. "I called you as soon as I..."

"Bullshit," she says. "You're leaving me."

"I don't want to. I have to," I say.

"You don't have to do anything," she says.

"We aren't eighteen yet, Mags," I remind her. "Otherwise, I would stay. I would say let's move in together. Let's stay together. Always."

She shakes her head and wipes her eyes. "You can't leave."

I drop to my knees and grab her around the waist, choking back tears. "I don't want to leave. I love you. You're the only thing that matters to me."

And then the sobbing starts. Her hands cover her eyes and her blonde hair falls over her shoulders. I never wanted to hurt her. Ever. But somehow here we are.

"Maggie, please. Let's stay together. It'll only be long distance for a little while. I'll find a way back here. To you. I promise."

"And when are you gonna come back? How?" she asks. Her eyes are stained with tears and the pain is palpable. It hurts me, too.

"Maggie..."

"That's what I thought. Goodbye, Alan. I'll always love you, you know?"

"I'll always love you, too, Maggie."

PART THREE

NOW

TWENTY-THREE

I AM STILL WAITING for Alice to call me. At this point, I've jerked off once and fucked Sabrina twice. The sun is starting to go down and I wonder if that will make Alice return to me. Maybe she only misses me when it's dark. Maybe she only misses me when she's drunk. But I can't think about that. I can't. Because I can't accept it. I won't. I need her.

I walk into the kitchen and the shot glass is still on the counter. I pour the whiskey into it and throw it back. I repeat this three times until my throat burns but in the way that I need it to. The way that will soothe me. The way that will soothe this. The way that might make it all bearable.

I think about Sam. And Jenny. But mainly Alice. I've tried to call her three times today and texted twice but fuck it. I pick up my phone and dial her number. It rings until it goes to voicemail and I hear her sweet voice in my ear. I text her.

"Please call me," I send.

But I know she won't. So I call her again.

"Hello?" she asks, like it's a question.

"Alice, I got your text last night. I miss you, too. Please, come over. Let's talk about this," I say.

"No," she says. And then she says it again but firmer this time. "No. I'm sorry. That was a mistake. I'm not coming over. We're done, Alan. Please, just stop calling me. Don't make this any harder than it has to be."

"But Alice..." I start. And the click on the other end is deafening.

I throw my phone into the living room. I pour another three shots. Drink them down. Feel sorry for myself. I miss Alice. I miss everything we had.

And then, I'm mainly thinking about Jenny. How I made her feel without meaning to. How I made her feel something that's probably similar to this, even if it isn't as involved. Even if we never dated. Even if we never got anywhere close to saying I love you. Facts are facts. And I just want to feel good again.

I walk into the living room and pick up my phone. And I send Jenny a text.

"Hey..."

It beeps about a minute later. "What's up," she says.

"Nothing. Just home, hanging out. Kinda think I owe you an apology. Wanna come over?"

"Grrr. You are so annoying."

I don't answer. Ten minutes later I get another text.

"I'll be there in fifteen minutes," she says.

I clean up around the apartment a bit. I put the coffee mug I set out for Alice in the sink and wash it. Because she never came. She isn't coming. But Jenny is. I pick up Sabrina and put her away, making sure she is safely tucked into the closet. No trace of her around. I make the bed as neatly as I can. It'll do. I'm sure Jenny doesn't care. But I do wish I could wash my sheets so they would stop smelling like Alice. Alice is gone. Done. I need to let her go. I need to move on. And I need to be fair and give Jenny a real shot. No one should feel like this.

Twenty minutes later and there is a quiet knock on my door. I'm about to yell for her to come in but decide I should greet her at the door. She deserves to have the door opened for her. So I do.

And when the door opens, freeing up the space between us, her brown eyes are looking at me with curiosity.

"Hey," I say. "Come on in."

I can feel her roll her eyes even though I'm looking at the back of her head now as she walks past me and inside. "I'm surprised you invited me over after I freaked out and left," she says.

"You had every right to," I say. "You were right. I was being a dick. And I really am sorry."

She's in the kitchen now, eyeing the shot glasses and the bottle. "Did you have people over earlier?"

"No, just me," I say. "You want a drink?"

"Might as well, right?" she says, sliding two of the shot glasses over to me, and grinning.

"That's right," I say. I walk over, but the bottle is in front of her. She leans against the counter in front of it and smirks at me. She wants me to get it with her in the way. Her tits are sticking out of her shirt the more she leans back and she needs to stop before I rip her clothes off right here and be a dick all over again. I smile. "Can you pass me that, please?"

She sighs. "Fine. Here. You're no fun." She turns around and picks up the bottle then hands it to me.

I pour us each a shot and look at her. "To forgiveness?" I ask.

Her face softens for the first time since she got here. "To forgiveness," she says, and we cheers and drink them down. She shakes her head after and makes a face, like some women do when a drink burns too much for their liking.

I fight a small smile. But my face becomes serious again while I'm watching her avoid my eyes. "I really am sorry."

She's fidgeting in her bag for something, probably her cigarettes. "You already said that," she says. "You don't have to keep apologizing. I already forgave you."

But she won't look at me for some reason. "Hey," I say, lifting her face with my hands so her eyes meet mine. "I mean it. I've been feeling like shit since my girlfriend dumped me. I'm sorry if I ever made you feel like shit. Okay?"

She looks into my eyes and nods. "Alan, it's fine. Like you said, before last time, we only had that one drunken night together. I just, I really liked that stupid drunken night. And then, I don't know, I thought maybe it'd be different if when we saw each other again we weren't hammered. If we weren't strangers anymore."

"We aren't strangers anymore," I say.

"We aren't?" she asks.

"Nope."

"Okay. Good. And for what it's worth, I'm sorry I went crazy on you. I just, I really did feel used. It isn't a good feeling. But you wouldn't know what that's like."

"Actually I do know what that's like."

She laughs. "Sure."

I pour myself another shot and ask if she wants one.

"Sure," she says. Only there's no mock in her voice this time.

We drink our shots and then I light a cigarette and light hers, too when she sticks one in her mouth.

"So, she really dumped you, huh?" she asks.

"Yup. She really did."

"Because of me?"

"For some reason, she thinks I cheated on her with you. I have no idea why. It's just so weird."

"That is weird. Are you okay? I don't want you to feel like shit about it."

"Eh, I do, but I'll be all right."

We smoke our cigarettes mostly in silence after that. I don't know what to say. Apparently she doesn't either. I pour myself another shot and gesture the bottle toward her to ask if she wants another and she nods. We repeat the routine. I pour. We cheers. We drink. She nervously smiles. I give a little smile back. It makes her smile more.

"You have the cutest dimples," she says.

I'll never understand why women love them so much but every time they say that, I'm grateful that at least my father gave me something. At least he gave me those fucking things. "Thanks," I say. And she's looking at me with that face. The face that says she wants me to rip her clothes off now. But I can't make the first move. Not after last time. Not after the way she blew up.

"You gonna kiss me or what?" she asks.

I make a face. "What kind of guy do you think I am?"

She moves closer to me and stands on her tip toes so she can throw her arms around my neck and press her body into mine. "I think I know what kind of guy you are. At least, to a certain extent."

"Oh yeah?" I ask. "And what kind of guy is that?"

"The kind of guy who gave me one of the best orgasms of my life," she says.

I gasp in mock shock. "Are you using me?" I ask.

She laughs. "Shut the fuck up." And then she kisses me.

TWENTY-FOUR

THE BED FEELS empty even though Jenny is right next to me. Her legs aren't draped over me. Her arms aren't touching me. I get up after we finish even though she's sleeping. I walk into the kitchen and pour myself another shot and sit at the kitchen table. I drink it down. Light a cigarette.

Jenny is a ghost of someone I thought she could be. Would be. Might be. I used a condom this time even though I didn't use one last time and at this point I don't think she really cares. I don't know if I do either. What's the point anymore? Of any of it?

I pour myself another two shots and get ready to get back in bed. I think of Sabrina in the closet. Tucked away. Hiding. She doesn't care if it feels good. Doesn't care if anything feels good.

I finish my cigarette and crawl back into bed with Jenny. I throw my arm over her and pull her close. I want the body heat. The comfort. The safety. Something. Anything to replace Alice and the emptiness she left behind.

· · ·

I guess I must have fallen asleep. Because I'm awoken by a voice. A familiar voice, a mad voice. A betrayed voice.

"What the fuck?" the voice cries. It's Alice's voice.

I jump up, sleepy-eyed and still half-drunk and now confused. I look next to me and Jenny is sitting up, naked, breasts exposed until she pulls the blankets up over them.

And then my eyes meet Alice's. She has never looked at me like this – so angry, so loveless.

"You fucking liar," she says.

I'm out of bed in my boxer briefs and running after Alice as she storms out of the room. "Alice, it's not what it looks like."

She whips her head around like it will be the final move she ever makes toward me. "*Don't.*"

I'm frozen. Her death glare has chilled me and I can't respond.

"God, I came here to tell you I was sorry. I'm such an idiot," she says, laughing to herself.

"No, you aren't. Listen, I..."

"There is no more listening," she says, twisting the knife. "Who is she? Let me guess. Jenny?"

I swallow because I feel the urge to throw up. I'm too much of a coward to say yes and I don't have to because my lack of response is her answer.

She shakes her head. "Want to tell me again how you didn't cheat on me with her? How it's not what it looks like? Because I think it's *exactly* what it looks like."

"I didn't cheat on you with her. I swear to god I didn't."

She's heading for the door and I'm following her because I can't let her leave. "Can we please just talk about this? She's only here because I thought we were done. You made it pretty clear you didn't want to see me, didn't want to hear me out. This, this is not cheating. You can't cheat on someone you no longer have."

"Yeah, you're right about that. You don't have me anymore. And you will never have me again," she says. Tears are running down her cheeks.

What time is it? I feel disoriented. Like this must be some sort of dream. A nightmare. Her hand is reaching for the doorknob and I'm watching it all unfold in slow motion. And I say the only thing I can think of. "Please don't go."

"You bastard. I wish I never met you," she says, and slams the door behind her.

My eyes are burning. My throat is dry. My chest is heaving. My hands are shaking. This can't be happening. I want to go back in time. I want to un-invite Jenny over. I want to give me and Alice another chance. The chance we deserved. I want to rewind the clock and have Alice walk up the stairs, into my apartment, and find me here, alone, sleeping. Missing her. Wanting her back. Willing to do anything to make it happen. I look fucking guilty. Like an asshole. A cheater. A liar. I'm mentally kicking my own ass when Jenny's voice interrupts me.

"Is that the only reason I'm here?"

I turn around and she's standing in the living room, sheet covering her naked body, pulled up to her breasts and wrapped around her torso. I look at her with a blank face, no expression. I am not up to any more arguing right now. I will let her say what she wants to, let her have her way with me. Let her tear me to shreds, too.

"Well?" she asks. "I think I at least deserve an answer."

No answer is your answer, Jenny. And the truth hurts, because she's wearing it now, too.

"You really know how to make a girl feel like shit," she says. "It's not a very good trait." She picks up the sheets that fall around her feet and walks like some sort of mummy to the bedroom where I'm assuming she's now getting dressed as fast as possible. At least this time she isn't throwing things or yelling.

I look around. It's early in the morning. It's light out. The sun has risen. That means that Alice still missed me when the sun came up. That means I blew it, for the last time.

I hear Jenny stomping around in the bedroom. She's getting dressed, clumsily. Probably still half-drunk as well. She finally comes out, makeup smeared, hair tied in a bun, wearing her clothes from yesterday, and I hate myself for looking at her and thinking of her as a mistake. I really am an asshole.

"Do us both a favor," she says, voice flat. "Never call me again just because you're lonely. Because you can't have the girl you actually want. I'm not okay with being someone's second choice."

And I don't respond. I don't try to defend myself or argue with that statement, because she's right. And because, to put it quite simply, if I'm being honest with myself, I just have no more fight left in me.

TWENTY-FIVE

I SLEEP OFF THE MORNING, most of the day and into the night. I finally get up to shower and try to wash this all off me, but it doesn't work. I am still dirty. Still alone. Still without Alice. And I never thought that two different women would break me in the same day, but they did. And they were good, Jenny especially.

Alice, I love her. She didn't need to do much to destroy me other than tell me she didn't want me anymore. But for Jenny, well, it's hard to hurt someone who doesn't really care much about you. But, I did care. She got me to care. Once I saw in her face how hurt she was. Once I saw my patterns materialize into her. Once I saw how I could affect someone without even knowing or thinking they would be affected.

She made me feel like less than a man and more like the scumbags I try to protect drunk women from at bars at 2am. Me. Am I one of those guys? A guy a girl should be protected from? A guy who would take advantage of women? Drunk or sober? I fucking hope not. I really hope not. I don't want to be a bad guy. I walk into the kitchen and wash my hands. I dry my hands then look at the bottle on the counter and grip it as I lift it, picking up a shot glass with my other hand. I tilt the bottle until the liquid is just about to run from the opening, and I stop. I put the bottle down. I put the shot glass down. I don't want to be like my father. What I want is to get Alice back.

If I was that close to getting Alice back, I think I still have a chance. She can't be mad at me for hooking up with Jenny after she had already broken up with me. Well, she could. But she couldn't hold it against me. I was technically single. So was she. And I wouldn't be happy if she fucked someone else, but, what could I do? I could choose to get over it because I love her or I could choose to picture her with this other guy for the rest of my life. I'd choose her, every time. Every fucking time.

I slip on my work boots and pick up my phone. It's 7:48pm. It's still early enough. I know if I have any god damn chance of getting this woman back, I need to get off my ass and do something. There's something called the "grand gesture" that Alice likes to talk about, especially during movies when the guy fucks up. She always says they'll never go back, "unless he does some sort of grand gesture or something". Whatever this grand gesture is that they want probably depends on the woman. But with Alice, I know her. I know what it will take to convince her that I'm serious. That I love her. That I want to be with her and only her.

At least I think I know. I'm getting hard and stressed just thinking about this. I take Sabrina out of the closet, even though I really only have time for a quickie. I don't even take her top off this time, I just pull it down until one of her silicone tits pop out so I can grab it before I pull up her skirt and fuck her. I grip her hair as I'm thrusting, and I pull it harder right before I finish.

I clean us both up then wash my hands and brush my teeth. I put on deodorant. I put on Alice's favorite cologne of mine. The one she says makes me smell "yummy" even though I used to like to remind her that "yummy" isn't an actual scent. What could have been a smile haunts my lips as I put Sabrina back in the closet, thinking of the way Alice would slap my arm when I'd say stuff like that.

And then I grab my wallet and phone and I'm off to the store. I know what I need to get. I grab two dozen roses from the store three blocks away and a bag of peanut M&M's. Then, I stop at the liquor store. I grab a bottle of Pinot Grigio, her favorite. And the weather is a little chilly but the adrenaline in me is warming me up so I walk. I have about a fifteen-minute walk from here to Alice's and I'm hoping she's home. I stick the roses under my armpit and take out my phone. Dial her number. She forwards me to voicemail. I grin, because she doesn't know it yet, but I do: Hope is not lost. Not yet. Not when we have the whole night ahead of us. Our whole lives ahead of us, just out of reach right now. But if she will just shift a little to the left, a little closer to my arms, we can fix this.

I reach her building and know I can't get in without her. I try calling her again. No answer. But I see her car down the block. She should be home. I text her.

"I'm outside," I send.

I have an iPhone. She has an iPhone. I stare at the screen waiting for the little fucking bubbles to appear. They don't. And she never has her "read" on.

"Please, come out. I have something for you."

Still no bubbles. I wait five minutes before sending another.

"I want to give you something. If you still don't want to talk to me or be with me, I'll accept that."

And I stare at the screen and brace myself for no bubbles. For the empty digital screen staring back at me silently laughing and mocking me about what a big failure this was. What a big failure I am. And I think about how much colder the walk home will be if she doesn't answer. If I'll have to leave all this stuff on her car. On her windshield. Or if she left her doors open like she usually does even though I tell her not to. Even though I tell her she needs to be careful because there are bad people out there. But no, not Alice. Alice likes to see the good in people. Maybe she likes to see it in everyone but me, now.

And I think I'm imagining things when I see the bubbles.

Bubbles?

Bubbles!

"I'll be down in five minutes," she says.

And there it is. *Hope.* In the form of a god damn text message, no less.

TWENTY-SIX

I AM STANDING HERE like an asshole, trying to balance the roses with the wine and the M&M's and I don't know what I'm going to say. I want to smoke a cigarette but Alice wouldn't like that. She doesn't like smoking. She doesn't like when I take seconds off my life meanwhile she's taking off minutes, weeks, years, with every second that goes by while I stand here, waiting for her, alone.

Eventually, the door opens and she appears like an angel. Here to save me. Here to accept what I've brought her.

Her 5"6 frame appears and closes the door behind her and she steps out but only onto the stoop. Not out onto the sidewalk where I stand. She looks at all the crap I have in my hands and I expected her to at least smile but she doesn't.

"What do you want?" she says, and it isn't even a question. It's an accusation.

"What do I want?" I ask. "I want you. I miss you. I love you, Alice."

I see her swallow and she crosses her arms. "You have a funny way of showing it."

I start nearing the stoop and she steps back, closer to the door than she was before.

"Look, I want to clear some things up. Once and for all. I met Jenny before I knew you. She was a one-night-stand. I got back in touch with her to try to see why you would think I cheated on her. Nothing happened with her while we were together. I would never cheat on you. Ever. I got with her again after you broke up with me. Because she wanted me and I fucking missed you and I couldn't have you so I had her. She was something to take my mind off of you. That's it. I hardly know her. At all."

"You slept with her, even though you say you missed me. You still slept with her," she says.

"You said you didn't want anything to do with me," I say. "You said that. Not me. Then you show up and get all mad that someone else is there. What do you want from me, Alice? I miss you, and I want to be with you, but if you tell me you don't want to be with me I can't just wait around feeling sorry for myself and be alone forever."

"It's been a few days, Alan."

"I deal with things differently."

"Obviously you do," she says.

"If I thought I had another shot with you I would have stayed alone," I say. "Here." I hand her the roses and the wine and the M&M's. "These are for you. Even if you never want to see me again, I want you to have these. And I want you to know that every time I see any of these things, I will always think of you. And I will always miss you."

She takes a few steps closer to me and stretches out her hands to accept the gifts. Her face softens. "Thank you." And I see her choking back tears.

"Alice, I love you. Just please, give me one more chance to prove it to you. There is no one else for me."

"I want to, Alan. I really do. But I can't trust you. Not after all this. Not after walking in on you with her. With *her*. The girl you swore you didn't cheat on me with. Like, are you kidding me? *The* fucking girl! You're unbelievable, you know that? I would have married your dumb ass."

"You should still marry me," I say.

She almost chokes on thin air. "Marry you? Really? I can't even think of spending the next ten minutes with you, Alan. I'm sorry. We're done. I appreciate the gifts. I really do. It's sweet of you. But I can't forgive you. I just can't. I hope you understand, but really, I don't need you to. I just need you to stay away."

"Okay. I'll stay away. But I'll always love you."

"Thanks," she says, and she turns around and opens the door and heads inside.

And I want to stop her. I want to run after her and grab her by her waist and fall to my knees and kiss her feet and beg her, literally fucking beg her, to trust me. To be with me. To let me show her how much I love her. To let me prove it to her. To let me be the man I know I can be for her. The man I am for her. The man she chose. The man she would choose every time. But I don't because she doesn't want me to. She doesn't want to hear it. Because she doesn't want to see my face ever again. She wants me to go away. To disappear. To have never existed at all.

Because she didn't choose me. Not this time. And I don't know how to fix that, because I can't. So instead I stare at the old beige door with the numbers 42. I look at her stoop, memorizing the cracks. I look at the gate, taking snapshots in my mind. I step back and look at the building. The door. The gate. The stoop. The empty stoop. The closed door. The lack of Alice on the sidewalk with me. And I close my eyes and remember her scent and watch mental flashbacks of our time together. And when I open them, she is still not here with me. She is gone. And I am alone. And if it's possible, I miss her more than I did before. And I'm fighting back tears because men don't cry. Not over stuff like this. Not in public.

Maybe my version of the grand gesture wasn't grand enough. Maybe I just underestimated her hatred of me now. It doesn't matter anymore. The walk home is going to be a lot colder than I thought it would be. I'll never get Alice back. I've ruined it. And I just want to feel good.

TWENTY-SEVEN

I AM WALKING HOME empty-handed without my girl on my arm because she's no longer my girl. Never will be again. I'm thinking about going home to fuck Sabrina until I pass out but it won't do. Not tonight. Tonight, I need a real woman. I need her warmth. Her legs around me. I need someone to kiss me back because they want to.

I make a left on 9th and head to the bar. It's early enough that everyone won't be shit faced yet, but I plan on getting pretty sauced myself. I need a drink. If Alice were here, she'd tell me that drinking won't make it hurt any less. And maybe she'd be right. But it sure as shit is going to help me forget for at least a little while. And that's all I really want right now.

I walk in and there's a guy playing acoustic guitar. I look over even though I already know who it is. Frankie Jones. I tip my hat to him and he nods. It's been too long since we've gotten together to bullshit and catch up. Frankie's a standup guy. He's had my back in quite a few scuffles, and vice versa. It's not often, but sometimes when he plays, guys get miffed at the way their girls look at him. His voice makes the ladies get all hot and bothered, and that leads to jealous boyfriends and sloppy punches.

I find an empty barstool and make my place at the bar. The bartender comes over. Jay.

"Sup, man?" he says.

I nod to him. "The usual."

"Heineken and Captain?"

"Yeah, please."

He puts the empty shot glass in front of me and pours the Captain in. Then he pops the cap off the Heineken and slides it to me. "Tab?" he asks.

I take my wallet out of my back pocket and hand him my card. "Run it."

Frankie's playing an acoustic version of "Let Her Cry" by Hootie and the Blowfish and I listen to it and want to fucking cry my damn self. I'm pathetic.

Frankie finishes off strong as I'm finishing my Captain. I feel his familiar slap on the back.

"Al! My man," he says.

I get up off the barstool to shake his hand. "What's up, Frankie? Sounding good up there, as usual."

"Thanks, man. Trying, anyway. We drinking the old Captain again tonight?"

"You know it," I say, taking my spot on my barstool again.

He takes the empty spot next to me and Jay heads over immediately. "Sup, Frankie? Killing it out there! What'll you have?"

"Thanks, Jay. I'll have what he's having," Frankie says, pointing to me. "And fill up his Captain, too."

Jay does his routine and leaves us to catch up.

"Cheers, Frankie," I say, holding my shot glass up to him.

And he clinks it. "To friendship, music, and chicks," he

says.

"It's been too long," I say. "What's new with you?"

"Shit. Just working, playing, trying to get a record deal. It isn't happening yet though."

Frankie's eyes are tired. I see the bags under them and I know he's busting his ass trying to make this dream a reality. "You got it, Frankie. Just keep putting yourself out there. Something is bound to give."

"Fucking better. I'm so broke, dude. Between paying for studio time and rent, I'm getting raped out here."

I wipe my hands together and I want to wash them. And part of me wants to tell him he shouldn't say shit like that. But he doesn't know better, people usually don't. They say shit like this and they don't know how it cuts some people, even when they don't mean it to. Even when they mean it as a joke. Frankie's a good guy. He just doesn't understand the implications of that word. Everything behind it.

"What's up with you? You holding up okay?" he asks.

"You heard?" I ask. I didn't tell him about Alice.

"Yeah, man. Fucking Jay, he's such a dick."

"Jay? What's he got to do with anything?" I ask.

"Dude, Alice came in here last open mic and I asked her where you were but she said it was a girls' night. Next thing I know, she's all pissy and leaves. I asked Jay what happened. I thought maybe some guy was hitting on her. I try to watch out for her when you're not here. Then Jay starts laughing, says he told her how you came here and got wasted and left with some chick named Jenny. The city slut, he called her. He told Alice this girl was the equivalent of the subway and everyone's had a ride. Including you. And that it seemed like you were getting off two stops at once."

I feel a surge of rage fill my entire body and without realizing it I'm clenching my fists so hard I think my fingers might snap. "Are you fucking kidding me? That's why Alice thinks I cheated on her?" I pick up my Heineken and chug it. "Frankie, I'm going to break his fucking face. I'm serious." Then I look over at him. "Jay," I call. It's not a yell, but it isn't a question either.

"Alan, calm down, man. Let's go outside and smoke a cigarette before you do anything. This is your favorite bar. You can't beat his ass in here."

Jay looks over and I recognize the look on his face. Fear. And it's justified. Because I'm going to kill him. Actually kill him. I picture myself bashing his face against the bar top and cracking his skull and his last words being a piss poor excuse for an apology.

"I'm gonna kill him," I say.

"Dude, come on. Let's go," he says. He's off his barstool and Jay is walking over. "Don't, Jay. Go back to whatever it is you were doing," he warns.

I don't know how Frankie does it but he pulls me off the barstool and to the door until we are standing outside and he sticks an already lit cigarette in my hand.

I smoke it. I concentrate on anything but the fact that Jay caused all of this. For no reason other than the fact that he's a dick. Because that's the kind of guy he is. Because that's how some guys are. And this is exactly why I don't trust most of them.

"Alan," Frankie says. "You good, man?"

I'm shaking I'm so angry. I know this is what comes before I beat the shit out of him.

Frankie is saying something. Words. I can't hear them. All I hear are my own thoughts. My own voice in my head. Telling me to go and find Jay. To hurt him. Badly. To do irreparable harm to him.

And then I see her. Jay's girlfriend. She's walking up the sidewalk with her friend toward the bar.

I stop shaking. And I smile. Without looking at Frankie, I say "I'm gonna fuck his girlfriend."

"That's bad karma, man," Frankie says.

I laugh. "Yeah? I'll fuck karma, too."

TWENTY-EIGHT

HER NAME IS Lindsay and she's cute. Too cute to be with an asshole like Jay. Frankie doesn't think I can manage to sway her but I know he's wrong. Lindsay is young. I don't know how young. Old enough to drink and date an asshole like Jay but too young to realize just how much of an asshole Jay is. I catch her off guard on the sidewalk.

As I pass her, I almost walk into her but I move. "Excuse me," I say, "but your boyfriend sucks." And then I keep walking.

"Wait, what'd you just say?" she calls.

But I just keep walking. A few moments later I hear her little feet running after me.

"Hey," she calls. And when I don't stop, "Hey!" She catches up to me and stops me by putting her hands on my arm.

I finally stop and look at her. "Sorry, but he does."

"You mean Jay?" she asks.

"Unless you have two boyfriends," I say, with a joke in my voice, because we both know I mean Jay.

But she doesn't laugh. She looks down for a moment, embarrassed. Then she looks back up at me. "What'd he do now?"

"Now?" I ask. I let out a small laugh. And I think about ignoring the question. But no. She deserves to know. She deserves to be in on this. I want this to be her payback as much as it is mine. "Now, he decided to tell my girlfriend I cheated on her."

"And you didn't?"

"And I didn't. I would *never* have cheated on her. But that doesn't matter now."

She looks down again. And I think she needs to stop looking down so much. I think that's a sign for women. Women who are not used to being treated well. Women who do not understand how much the look in their eyes is worth. Women who do not know what it means to be appreciated.

"Hey," I say. "Stop looking away. It isn't your fault he's a piece of shit."

And in those words, something moves her. Because her eyes change. And she's looking at me now. Not like a stranger. Not like a creep. But like someone who actually sees her for once. Someone who fucking gets it. And I do. I do get it.

"You wanna go to him or do you wanna come with me?" I ask. But we both know the answer as she latches onto my arm and squeezes. I look at her and smile. "Good choice."

"He sucks. He does," she says. "I know."

"He really does."

"I'm sorry."

"You don't have anything to be sorry for," I say. "You deserve better than him. But you know that, don't you?"

She nods.

"So why stay?" I ask. We've cleared the block. Another four to go.

"I don't know. Because it's better than being alone. That makes me pretty pathetic, huh?"

I shake my head. "Nope. It doesn't. Most people can't handle being alone. But being alone would beat the hell out of staying with that fucking guy."

"You're right."

"I know." And we both know I'm right. But right now, it isn't about me being right. It's about two things. Me, getting back at Jay the best way I can. The way that will piss him off almost as much as he pissed me off. And Lindsay, giving him one last parting present to remember her by.

She doesn't open up about anything he's done to her. But by the time we reach my apartment, she isn't as shy.

I open the door and let her go first. When we get to the top of the stairs, I unlock my door and open it for her.

Before the door fully closes I hear her taking off her jacket. I turn around and find her sitting on the kitchen table, holding my bottle of whiskey in her hands. She takes a swig then holds the bottle out. I guess she needs some bravery here.

"Hey," I say, walking over, accepting the bottle. I take a drink from it. "You gonna regret this? Because if you are, I don't..."

And she pulls me into her and wraps her legs around me. "Are you kidding me? You're fucking gorgeous," she says.

I smile. Then I take another swig. "You're definitely prettier than I am," I say.

She smiles and grabs the bottle from me and takes two gulps. I grab it from her hands and set it down on the table next to her. Far enough away that it won't knock over before I do what I'm about to do.

And I lean down and kiss her, gently pushing myself into her as she pulls me in harder. Wrapping her legs around me and tightening her grip. Moving her hips to meet me. To feel me. I lift her up and carry her into the bedroom, my right hand gripping her ass as I walk. She's moaning into my ear and kissing me. And I have her top off by the time we get to the bed. I toss her down on it, quick enough that she laughs and wants more. I go to the drawer to grab a condom. Because who the fuck knows where Jay has been. I trust her, but not him. And when I get the wrapper out and turn around she's on her knees with her bra off.

She's a little thing. Petite. Light. Tiny. And as I'm taking off my shirt, I know we're going to have fun with this.

I can't count how many positions I put her in. Or the way her eyes roll back the first time she orgasms. But I make her cum three times before we're done. And she says my name like she never even knew who Jay was. Like he never knew the meaning of making love to his woman. Like he never existed at all.

When we finish, she lazily turns to me, her blonde hair falling over her face. "Holy shit," she says. "That was good. *Really* good."

I light a cigarette and I smile. Her arm is over my chest.

And I probably just fucked Jay's girlfriend better than he ever did. It's the last thought I have before I fall asleep.

TWENTY-NINE

I WAKE up with Lindsay's thin arm slung over my chest and her leg over mine. She is spooning me, hard. I can't say I don't like it. I don't have to look down to know I'm already hard and I wonder if I should make her coffee or get her off. I don't know how she takes either in the morning, but I could guess. As I move, she rolls over onto her side and her bare back is exposed.

I can't help it now. There's something about a woman's back and her bare shoulders that make me insane. I slide the comforter down and put my hand on her hip and graze her thigh as I start kissing her back. Her shoulders. She responds with a moan and that's all I need. I'm grabbing her ass now with one hand and reaching for the nightstand drawer for a condom. I have it on before she even notices.

It's almost a surprise when I slip it in. Slowly. She responds beautifully, already wet and wanting. Women can't fake that. Desire. It's either there or it isn't. And if it isn't, you better question yourself. Because it's about her, not you. It is always about making her feel good. But most guys are selfish.

Like Jay. I'm sure he doesn't take the time to play with her breasts. Her ass. Tease her just enough to be ready for a climax before you even really start.

She screams my name loud enough that I worry what the neighbors downstairs will think. Afterwards, I kiss her on the lips and tell her she's gorgeous, just in case she forgot. Just in case she hasn't heard it enough in her life. In case Jay doesn't tell her. I am trying to remind myself that her warmth isn't meant to be a home, but it was nice while it lasted.

She gets up and gets dressed and I try not to watch her. She's shy now, in the mornings. Maybe a little embarrassed. It's endearing on her. But she smiles like a girl who doesn't know how incredible she is even when she isn't trying. And for a second, it breaks my heart and makes me want to love her.

But I get up and put my boxer briefs on. Then jeans. A white t-shirt. I throw a gray hoodie on because it's a little cold in here and I ask her if she wants one and she nods. Fuck. They're in the closet. Sabrina. So I take mine off and walk over to her. I tower over her little frame. And she puts her arms up and I slip the sweatshirt on over her. It's huge. Too big for her. And she looks so fucking cute in it that I pick her up and kiss her and grab her ass.

"You're fucking adorable, you know that?" I say. "Come on."

I go into the kitchen with her following me and I make us some coffee. I ask her how she likes it and she blushes.

"Light and sweet," she says.

"Just like you?" I say with a smile, because it's cheesy.

She laughs and says she guesses so.

I finish making her coffee first and hand her the mug which she accepts with a smile and a quiet "Thank you".

When I finish mine I sit at the table with her and I light a cigarette. I would ask if she wants one but she doesn't smoke. I only know that because she told me last night. But she never told me I tasted like an ashtray. So I take it she doesn't mind it.

"What do we do now?" she asks.

"We drink our coffee," I say, with a smile in my voice.

"Shut up, you know what I mean."

Oh. That. This. Us. Jay. "What do you want to do?"

"I don't know."

Ah, but she does know. She just won't tell me. I stay quiet. This usually does the trick. If you give a female some room to think out loud, she normally will.

"I know you just used me to get back at him," she says. "And that's okay. I sort of used you for the same thing. But, it *was* fun."

"It definitely was fun," I say, taking a drag of my cigarette and a sip of hot coffee.

"Do you want to see me again?" she asks.

I swallow the coffee and it kind of burns. Fuck. I think she thinks I'm her new Jay. Her new guy. To date? To fuck? "See you, how?" I ask. I need clarity. Women dance around topics they don't feel comfortable saying outright. I never understand it.

"Physically see me again," she says. "With your eyes. What do you mean how?"

And now I'm the one dancing around it because how do I delicately ask this? "I would love to see you again. But if you mean a commitment of any sort, I'm just not there right now. I *just* got out of a relationship. With a girl I thought I would marry one day. I'm not really in the right place mentally to give all of myself to someone right now."

"I'm not asking for marriage," she says, brown eyes

peeking out from behind the mug that looks huge in her little hands.

"I know that. I just don't want to lead anyone on right now. I don't want to be that guy."

"What kind of guy do you want to be?" she asks.

And the honesty in that question stuns me for a minute. And I would try to think of something clever to say but I'm coming up short. So I respond with the truth. "I don't know. The kind of guy who deserves the attention of a girl like you."

"Well, you've got it."

"Do you get to tell Jay or do I?" I ask.

"Why don't we let him see for himself?" she says with an evil little smirk. "He's working tonight."

"I like the way you think."

She smiles.

And we finish our coffee. And exchange numbers. She says she needs to go home and shower so I offer to walk her home but she decides to Uber. I insist on walking her downstairs when the Uber comes.

We get outside and I can tell she isn't sure if she should kiss me or not so I save her the trouble of worrying about that and kiss her once on the lips.

"Oh, let me give you this back," she says, starting to move to take my sweatshirt off.

"No," I say. "Keep that on. It's cold. You can give it to me later." I say it even though I know damn well I will never get it back. Sometimes I think women only like us for our hoodies.

She smiles and gives me a hug. "Thank you. I had a really nice time."

"I did, too. Call me when you're ready and I'll come and get you."

She says she will and then hops in the Uber. I watch

them drive off and look up at the sky. The sunlight doesn't hurt this time. The sky is clear. Blue. Not a rain cloud in sight. And the sunshine feels nice. Warm. Like Lindsay.

And for once I am not thinking about Alice and how much this sucks. I am thinking about how good this feels. I didn't just fuck Jay's girlfriend, I made love to her. And then I stole her. I hope he misses her like I miss Alice. But for some reason, I don't think he will. And that pisses me off for a minute before I remind myself I'm glad that loser will never get the chance to have Lindsay again. He never deserved her. But neither do I.

And the sadness hits me all over again.

And I go back upstairs into my apartment and take a long, hot shower.

THIRTY

I PICK Lindsay up at approximately 7:45pm because she decides she wants to "pre-game". She doesn't have the courage to do this sober. To walk in on my arm and look Jay in the face without a buzz. To tell him it's over and this is the way it ends. She is not typically a cheater. I can tell. There is an uncomfortable expression glued to her face like someone reminded her of me and then stuck it there. She doesn't kiss me when she sees me. Doesn't hug me. Doesn't do anything having to do with any sort of affection. She looks at me like I am the cancer.

We get to my apartment and she is not even shy anymore. She figures her morals have already been shot to hell, I guess. She is drinking the whiskey straight from the bottle as I finally interrupt her.

"Lindsay, you okay? You might want to slow down."

She laughs and almost coughs some of it up. "Right," she says. "*Slow down.* Now you want me to slow down?"

I don't know what that means but I don't want to inquire.

"I just think you should slow down on chugging the liquor. It's not even nine o' clock yet."

"Don't be a pussy," she says, taking another swig.

Lindsay might be a party girl. Maybe she's not drowning her sorrows. Maybe she just likes to get wasted. Nothing wrong with that. She is younger than me. Maybe she's just into the partying thing right now at this stage in her life. Maybe Jay made her want to get fucked up all the time. Maybe she *is* just drowning her sorrows. Maybe I pushed her here. Fuck. I don't know. All I know is I'm not a pussy. So I take the bottle when she passes it to me and I take a good drink of it.

Something in her changes then because she sits down and her face has softened. "I'm sorry. I'm just nervous."

Even though it was her idea, I give her an out. "You don't have to do this, you know."

"Do what?" she asks, looking up at me.

"Any of it. Go there. Tell Jay. Hell, if you don't want Jay to know, I won't say a word to anyone."

She thinks it over for a minute. Runs her hand through her perfectly straight blonde hair. "I just know Jay. He's gonna call me a slut. Wouldn't be the first time. I guess that's part of the reason I did it. He always accuses me of shit, talks about me in front of his friends like I'm not even there. I know it was wrong, but fuck him. Seriously. I should have dumped him when he called me a dumb slut in front of his friends."

I have to hide the rage seeping through my bones. The urge to kill him comes back all over again. Stronger. But I keep my voice calm. "Why didn't you?"

"Because I'm an idiot."

"Look at me." I have to repeat it twice before she finally picks her eyes up from the floor. "You're not an idiot. And you're not a slut. And you should never let any guy call you any of those things. Ever again. You hear me?"

She nods, but neither of us know if she will actually take my advice or not. The saddest thing of all is that women allow themselves to be spoken to this way. That they have allowed men to make them feel like they deserve it. That they even go as far as to apologize for it.

"If you want, I'll beat the shit out of him," I add.

She laughs a little. "No, please don't do that. He doesn't deserve that."

"Trust me, he does."

She shakes her head. "Please, promise me you won't hurt him?"

I feel my jaw lock and my mouth gets hard. "I can't promise that."

"Alan, please. This will hurt him enough. You beating the shit out of him won't accomplish anything."

Wrong. It could potentially stop him from treating people like this in the future. But I stay silent.

"Promise me," she says.

"I promise I'll try not to," I say. "It's the best I can do. But if he talks down to you in front of me, he's getting hurt. I promise you that."

A thick concern paints itself on her face and she tries to ignore it. "Last time I checked, I didn't hire you as my bodyguard," she says, crossing her arms with a playful look in her eyes.

"No, you didn't. I volunteered."

She smiles and takes a little sip from the bottle. "Come on, let's go and get this over with."

"You sure you want to do this?"

"Hell yeah," she says, sure this time. "Fuck him."

"That's the spirit," I say. I hold out my arm to her. "After you."

We get there around 9:45pm. As predicted, Jay is behind the bar serving drinks. She walks in holding onto my arm. I've got a Cubs cap on. Frankie spots us immediately and gets up from his barstool. He isn't playing tonight. I knew he wouldn't be. He gets one night a week.

He walks over to us, looking over his shoulder once to see if Jay caught us yet. "Alan, man," he says, shaking my hand. He looks at Lindsay and smiles the old Frankie smile. "Ma'am," he says.

She gives him a polite smile and blushes a little.

"What's up, Frankie?" I say, feeling like a smug bastard. I don't have to say I told him so – Lindsay on my arm says it for me.

Jay disappears from behind the bar. Lindsay notices. I notice. Frankie doesn't because his back is to the bar.

"Gonna be one of those nights, huh?" Frankie asks, seeing the looks on our faces.

"Just might be," I say.

"Dude, just don't get me banned from the one fucking bar I have a steady gig at, okay?" he says.

"Chill, I got it," I say.

Jay comes from behind and I hear his voice. "Alan, what the fuck, bro?"

I turn around, half expecting to get sucker punched. But I've got a few inches on the kid so I look down at him. "You wanna do this in here where all your buddies can see or you wanna take it outside?"

He looks at Lindsay and I can tell he wants to say something to her. Desperately. He's biting his tongue. His face is red from the anger. His cheeks flushing fury. And he's looking at her like he wants to call her a bitch or worse and it makes me want to kill him just for that. He responds by turning his back and heading for the door, pushing it open like he's got something to prove.

"Frankie, stay with her. Make sure none of Jay's friends give her a hard time," I say.

Lindsay pulls on my arm. "You promised."

"I said I'd try," I said. I pick up her hand and kiss it. "Stay with Frankie." Then I'm out the door before she can say another word.

We're on the sidewalk now. Jay is pacing like the little rat he is.

"You got something you wanna tell me?" I ask, giving him a chance.

"Dude, you fucking show up here with *my* girlfriend and you're asking me if *I* want to say something to *you*? What the fuck is this?"

People walking on the sidewalk are eavesdropping. Noticing. Looking. Watching. There isn't a crowd forming but they're walking slower. Taking their time to pass us.

I walk closer to him so he can hear me correctly. And I grab his shirt so he understands that I will kill him if he moves. "Let me tell you what the fuck this is. You told Alice that I cheated on her, which was a lie. You told your little buddies that Lindsay was a dumb slut, which was another lie. So guess what, Jay? You just lost your girl, too. Only difference is you deserve it." I let go of his shirt and shove him away at the same time.

"You fucked my girlfriend, didn't you?" he says. It's not a question. We both know I did. I guess he just wants to hear it.

I lean down and even my voice. "I didn't just fuck your

girlfriend. I fucked her better than you ever could. So since you like to run your mouth, you can tell people that, too."

He stands there, unmoving. Unflinching. Rage in his eyes. Probably unparalleled to mine though. Every ounce in my being wants to destroy him on the sidewalk and leave his body there for everyone to see. I wait to see if he's going to make a move. To see if he would dare try to hit me. But he won't. He's all talk. If a guy runs his mouth, it's because his hands aren't as quick.

As expected, he straightens out his shirt and goes inside.

THIRTY-ONE

I HAVEN'T HAD solid work in weeks and I'm beginning to feel useless. But having money helps. And when you work your whole life, and then can't because an actual fucking truck hits you, you get used to it. You almost look at it like an early retirement, because there's no other way really. When you work manual labor and then can't, you need to figure out a way around it to work off the books, or, get a job where you can basically sit on your ass all day. That's just not for me. One day I'm sure it'll have to be. But that day is not today. Not yet.

Today I have a job again. Painting and odd jobs for some loaded couple in Mendham. A guy I used to work with hooked me up. So I get in my truck and drive almost an hour to get there. I put the address in my GPS. Not too bad for a few days of work, a week or two at most. When I pull in to the circular driveway and look up at the house, Trevor wasn't kidding. These people really are loaded. It's an English colonial style basically fucking mansion with three levels, at least. Plus a basement and probably an attic. I grab my toolbox and turn my phone on silent then slip it into my pocket.

I walk up the baby smooth driveway to the front door and ring the doorbell, surprised there isn't a gate out here. A woman answers the door. Mid 40's I assume. Attractive. As hell. She's undoubtedly had her tits done because they're too big and perky to be real. And botox, I assume. Because her face looks fresh. Too fresh. Her makeup is flawless and she probably has less wrinkles than I do.

"You must be Alan!" she says, opening the door to the foyer. "Come in. Please pardon any mess. The housecleaners are due tomorrow."

I tell her it's no problem as I walk inside. Marble floors. Expensive custom furniture. A house straight from Good Housekeeping Magazine. Mess, my ass. I could eat off this floor and probably would.

She makes small talk. About her mostly. It's a big house for only two now that their kids are grown. Her husband wants the second office painted first. They're remodeling the second floor. She shows me the colors and I know he's picked them out despite her complaining.

"I told him it should be mauve, but he doesn't listen to me. He wants it gray. Of all things, could you imagine? Gray. I picked out these options and he chose gray over Glistening Silver Sand. Who does that?"

Rich people problems. I can't imagine as I shrug. Gray seems fine to me. Who wants silver glitter in their office?

She shows me the supplies her husband bought and it's fine. Rollers. Primer. He's got it covered. For a lawyer, he at least has the basics down. I thank her and try to get her out of there.

"Do you want a sandwich or anything?" she asks, leaning

her slim and toned body in the doorway against the entrance, curling a perfectly manicured finger around her blonde hair.

"I'm okay, thanks." I give her a polite response so she goes away. But she doesn't.

"You need a hand? It's a big room."

"Nah, I've got it. Thanks though."

A subtle hint of disappointment spreads across her face and she finally leaves, but not before asking if I want any water or tea or whatever it was that she was rambling about that she learned of in her yoga class yesterday. Something that helps you detox some bullshit. Lady, I don't fucking care. That's what I want to say. Just please leave.

She finally does. And I get to work. I get the primer ready and get to work on the first wall. The room is empty, so that's good. Usually people leave everything in there like they think you're a magician. And you have to work around everything. I suppose the help did that for them. When you have enough money you can do anything.

She comes back in a few hours later. I have the first coat done after the primer and it's looking good.

"I insist," she says, bringing a bottle of water.

I walk over to accept it. "Thank you."

"You sure you don't want anything for lunch? You've been up here for..."

"No, I'm fine, really. If I get hungry I'll go grab something. I appreciate it though."

"Nonsense, I'll make you a sandwich," she says, smiling.

These housewives get so lonely. I blame the husbands. Isn't it enough that they give you these big ass houses to live in? You don't have to work. You just get to sit home and do whatever you want. Why are they all so sad all the time?

She leaves the room and I get back to painting. I can already tell this job isn't going to work. She's too lonely and too hot. I'm too single and horny. I remind myself that this is a job. Work. But she comes back in the second time wearing a tank top and she knows what she's doing. These women are used to getting their way.

I hear the knock in the entryway and I know it's her. Before I turn around I prepare myself for whatever is on the platter. She might be naked for all I know. But when I turn it's her, in her workout clothes now. Holding a plate with a sandwich on it.

"Please, eat," she says.

I put the roller down and walk over to accept the plate. "Thank you. You didn't have to."

"I know," she says. "I wanted to. I appreciate you doing this on such short notice."

Cleavage. Her tits are too perky and she's gorgeous. I would wonder if she had kids if she didn't already mention them ten times, if I didn't see the pictures of them when I entered the house. They're everywhere on the walls. And they're grown. She's definitely not old but she's old enough to have kids who have left the nest. Kids who are off to college, at least. But fuck, she's hot.

Her green eyes are watching me and her hands are on her hips then in her hair and she's biting her lip now. "Trevor didn't say how old you were," she says.

She has a thing for younger guys. I don't know why. She just does and it's just making that obvious. But I'm not that young anymore. "32," I say.

"Oh, that explains why you seem like you know what you're doing."

"Yes, ma'am." I finish the first half of the sandwich in four bites. Anything to occupy my time. My mouth. My hands.

She looks from my face to the plate and laughs. "Seems like you were pretty hungry after all, huh?"

I nod and let out a "mm hmm" as I finish the second half of the sandwich. Then I hand her back the plate. "Thank you. That was really good."

She pulls on the top of her shirt and fans herself. "You're most certainly welcome. Is it a little hot in here?"

When you do that, yes. "No. I think it's fine."

"Well, the air has been tricky lately. If you get hot, feel free to come downstairs in the back. I think I'm gonna go for a swim. I wouldn't mind the company."

I nod. And she turns to leave wearing these fucking yoga pants or leggings or whatever girls call them. All I can see is her ass. And fuckkkkkkkk. She's good.

I remind myself of the job I need to do as I watch her walk away. I can feel my dick getting hard and I think about painting. I look at the shit in front of me. At how much I still have to do. I need to do at least one more coat. And I get back to work.

About another two hours pass by before she reappears. I have one more wall to do. Another hour or two. Her hair is wet. She's in a towel. Fuck, no.

"How's it going up here?" she asks.

"Good, I'll be finished up here in an hour or two. How was your swim?"

"Lonely, but nice nonetheless," she says. "I'll be in the master shower if you need anything. Anything at all."

I nod. Fuck. I'm used to the way some women throw themselves at me, but it's usually in less obvious ways. She drops the towel and starts to use it to dry her hair right there in front of me. Her bikini is revealing. Too revealing. I see the shape of her breasts as she bends over and I get hard but I pretend I don't and I turn. I should fuck her, now. In this room. Bend her right over this short ladder I have. This is work, I remind myself. But her ass cheeks are popping out of that too-small bikini bottom and oh my fucking god, woman.

I nod to her. "Sure thing."

I can see the look on her face. She knows she has me. Right where she wants me. A man with less self-control would take her right here. But I got this job referred to me by a friend. I can't. She leaves the entryway and my dick is so hard I want to say fuck this and leave. But I don't.

I start to think of something terrible to get rid of my boner. Then I remember Trevor. That this is a job. But that ass.

I finish painting while stroking the paint like I'd lick her body. Two hours later, I finish. Not in the way I want to. But I grab my things. I'm dirty. Paint all over my clothes from wiping my hands on my jeans. From measuring. From getting rid of the tape. From putting everything back in order. And I go downstairs to make a quick exit, but she's in the kitchen.

"Alan," she calls.

I was so close to the door. So fucking close. I turn around.

"This is for you," she says, handing me an envelope with cash in it. I don't have to open it to know it's cash. "For working so hard today."

"Thank you," I say. "I hope you enjoy the rest of your day."

She slides her finger over my arm. "I hope you enjoy yours, too." And she's too close to me. Looking up at me like she wants me to kiss her.

"Thank you," I say. And I turn. And I exit. And I walk to my truck like the fucking building might explode.

And I drive home, for almost an hour. And when I get home, I pull Sabrina out of the closet. And I close my eyes and imagine she's Mrs. Bikini and I fuck her until I cum so hard I fall asleep right after.

THIRTY-TWO

ONCE YOU FANTASIZE ABOUT SOMEONE, even once, it's over. You're doomed. There's no hope for you. Even if you want to be celibate. Even if you want to do the right thing. It's most likely going to go the way you don't intend it to. But, of course, it's probably because somewhere in your subconscious, your desires are stronger than your will to refuse those desires. And me, I'm weak. I wake up, fully, knowing I'm a dead man, and I get out of bed. Sabrina is still lying there. I put her away and I wash my hands. I make coffee.

I think about all the ways I do not want to fuck Mrs. Bikini but I also think about all the ways I could. I stop my thoughts because these, these fucking thoughts, they are what will lead to my demise. I need to be strong. Not only for myself, but for Trevor. He got me this job. I cannot and will not have sex with his client's wife.

I am making coffee while making promises to myself. I will be a good boy. I will be a good boy. I will be a good boy. I jerk off and fuck Sabrina, switching between the two. I take a shower. I get in my truck and I leave. I stop at the gas station off the highway and grab a pack of cigarettes.

I pull up to the almost-mansion in Mendham and park my truck in the driveway. I am thinking about her before I open the truck door. She is probably at least fifteen years older than I am but I wonder what she'll be wearing as I walk up to the door. This is my first mistake and I know it. I'm already thinking about her. Fantasizing comes first, thinking about her comes next. And after that...

I ring the doorbell. She gave me $500 cash yesterday for no reason other than the fact that she wants me. It was polite but it was a move. A power play. We both know it. And I hate myself because she's got the upper hand here. I'm fucking weak. I will be a good boy. I will be a good boy. I will be a good boy.

The door opens and she's wearing a towel. A fucking towel. A light pink towel that probably cost more than my entire living room set because it looks so soft and fluffy. And she's holding it at the center. And I can see the shape of her breasts beneath the plush fabric.

"Alan," she says, with feigned surprise in her voice. "I didn't expect you so early. I was just getting dressed. Please, come in."

She moves to let me in but doesn't give me much room. I just nod. "Early start." I try to slide past her like a fucking ninja without touching her. I will be a good boy. God, she smells good. Like fresh linens and soap. Hair conditioner. Perfume. A shower from sex heaven.

She closes the door behind me. I can feel her eyes on me and I feel like a pool boy or something. She's watching me. I hope she doesn't notice my dick starting to get hard but something tells me she might be looking.

"How was your drive over here?" she asks.

"Oh, it was fine. The traffic wasn't bad. Which room do you want me in next?" I ask. Shit. No. That came out way too wrong.

She laughs. She caught it. "The guest bedroom," she says. "Follow me." And she smiles at me. And she makes her way to the spiral staircase.

I'm staring at her ass under that towel and she knows it. She starts hand drying her hair as she walks, slowly, deliberately, up the stairs. This is fucking torture as I move my eyes from her ass to her back and shoulders and then to her legs. She's all tan and wet and lean and fuck me, here, on the stairs.

I fix my cap on my head and walk up the stairs with a purpose. I avert my eyes. I look at the ceiling. The railing. Anything. One step at a time. This is a job. Focus.

She makes it to the guest bedroom and points in. "Oh, there's a bed in the way. We won't be needing that, will we?" she asks, smirking.

Ignore it, Alan. "No, ma'am. I can move it when I need to get to that wall, don't worry." Please, dick, stop getting hard.

"Vivienne," she says.

"What?"

"My name is Vivienne," she says.

I swallow and look at the paint buckets set up with the rollers and everything else I need. "Okay, Vivienne. I got it. Don't worry. I'll just get to work in here. I'll make it as pretty as the rest of the house. Promise."

She laughs. Her smile, it's gorgeous. "You want any help? I'm not much of a painter but I think I could do it without getting too in the way. Charles wouldn't let me. I insisted, but he said I'd just make a mess."

Fuck, she's lonely. Too lonely. Too beautiful to be this lonely. "Tell you what, let me get the primer down and then if you want, you can help with the finish. I'm sure you won't make a mess of anything."

She lights up like someone just told her she won Miss America or something. "Really!"

I can't help but smile. "Yes, really. Just don't tell your husband or he'll feel cheated."

"I would never tell!" she says. "I'll just go and get dressed."

And she leaves the room. And I get to work on the primer.

A few hours later, after her checking in periodically, I tell her it's ready for her. She's dressed now, thank god. And she doesn't mean to, but she looks cute. Too cute. Overalls. A white t-shirt underneath. Her hair in a messy bun on the top of her head. Barefoot. She's been wanting to do this. Been wanting to be useful. Her sex kitten attitude changes and she is all business now, all about helping. Being "useful" as she calls it. And I want to kill her husband for making her think she was anything less than "useful" for something, or everything.

She's a chatterbox the whole time. Tells me where she grew up. Just over in Chester. Grew up horseback riding. The roads were dirt roads back then, she says. We'd never understand. All these malls replaced all the land. You could go out drinking with your friends and go to the store for pop and candy when you were kids. All in the same town. All with no malls. She hates how things are now. All technology and no heart. All pharmacy and no romance. I think I want to kiss her now more than ever.

And now that she's opened up, she blushes when I look at her. When she says something that makes me smile or laugh.

"God, I'm sorry," she says. "I must be so annoying. Just let me know if you want me to get out of your hair."

"Don't be sorry. You're not annoying at all. It's nice to have the company," I say. Another woman apologizing for another thing she never did wrong.

She's got paint all over her overalls and arms and hands now. Even a little on her face when she sneezed and wiped her nose. "I probably look like such a mess."

And I stop painting and look at her from the ladder I'm on. "Then you're one hell of a pretty mess, I'll tell you that."

Her face changes. She smiles. And she dips her brush back into the paint in the roller and gets back to work.

We break for lunch and eat a few sandwiches. A few hours later, we finish. The guest bedroom is a pretty yellow. Her choice this time. It's cheery but pale and glowing just like she is. She wipes her hands on her overalls and this time she doesn't have a tip for me in the form of an envelope.

"Thanks for today," she says, as she follows me to the front door.

"Oh, no. Thank you," I say. "You didn't have to help. I feel like I should split the profits with you."

She laughs. "Don't be silly. You were the one hired here, not me."

And this one, I don't know what to do with this one. This version of this woman that is not throwing herself at me. This woman who is sixteen all over again, standing before me in her own home, waiting to be kissed goodnight by the prom date. Only I'm not dropping her off. I'm not anything. I fight back every urge I have to kiss her then. Her green eyes looking up at me in sincerity. In hope. In appreciation.

"Enjoy the rest of your day, Vivienne. I'll see you tomorrow."

And then I let myself out before I take her in my arms and show her how beautiful she is. How wanted she is. How god damn irresistible and perfect she is.

PART FOUR

THEN

THIRTY-THREE

I WAKE UP. It is my 18th birthday. My mom and aunt have blue balloons everywhere for me. And two presents. One is a cake, baked by my mother. The other is a set of car keys on the counter. Wrapped in aluminum foil.

I only know what it is when I open it. And I look at my mother with a questioning glance.

"Happy birthday, baby. You've been wanting to go see Maggie. So, take my car. I know you're still saving up."

And she's right. I've been working part-time as a dish-washer at Luigi's, and at the auto shop helping out with the cars. I ask her if she's sure. She tells me to blow out the candle first and then decide. And I do. And I do.

I'm going to get Maggie back.

I got my license when I turned seventeen. I paid for the hours. I paid for the lessons. I paid for everything, almost in blood. Basically in blood. These people don't know what it means to be seventeen and horny, to need the love of your life. The girl who can smile and change everything in that one instance.

I give my mother a kiss on the cheek and hug her. We started doing that occasionally, when the time was right. "Thanks, Mom. I love you."

"I love you, too, honey. Happy birthday," she says. "Go get your girl."

I smile and we eat a piece of cake. And then I am getting dressed. I am putting on cologne and wondering if this flannel shirt still fits because it feels snug around my arms but it doesn't matter. I'm going to get Maggie. I kiss them both goodbye and get in the car. But not until I brush my teeth. Take a shower. Wash my hands twelve times.

I stop at the local store to get flowers for Maggie and I wonder if she will expect me. If she remembers that it is my birthday. And I drive the 122 miles to get to her. The highway is long and full of promise. The sun is shining. The sky is clear. Everything looks like it's meant for this. Meant for me, for us. Meant for redemption and all the things we could have had if time and circumstance didn't steal them away from us.

I pull up at her house. It looks the same. The paint on the outside hasn't changed. Her father's old Chevy is still parked in the driveway. I wonder if she has a car yet. If she drives. If she misses me. The beige of the house is fading and old and the curtains look like they haven't been changed in years. They still need a new roof. They still need to pave this old driveway.

And I walk up the driveway with my flowers in hand and I ring the doorbell, smoothing over my hair that is now long. Down to my shoulders. And I hope I don't look like a disappointment. I hope I still look like someone she wants. Someone she needs. Someone she once wrapped her arms around and said she'd love forever.

Her father comes to the door. He opens the door wearing

a gray t-shirt and a pair of jeans. His work boots are on even though it's a Saturday. A look of surprise and concern washes over him. "Alan? Is that you?"

"Hi, sir. Yes, it's me. Is Maggie home?"

"I thought you moved?" he asks. The shock is still hitting him I suppose. He looks like he's seeing some sort of ghost. And in a sense, I guess he is.

"I did, sir."

"Maggie is..."

"Dad? Who's there?" I hear her call. Her sweet voice comes from somewhere down the hall and I wonder if she still has her old bedroom. The one we used to make love in before her parents came home. And for a second, I wonder where her mom is.

My heart is thumping and all I can think of is what I'm going to say next. How I'll pick her up and swing her around when I see her and tell her I told her so. That I'd come back for her. That I am back. For her and only her.

John comes to the door.

John? My oldest friend, John?

"Alan!" he says, bringing me in for a hug. "Man, it's so good to see you! We've missed you around here!"

"John?" I ask out loud. I don't hug back. "What are you doing here?"

It must strike him in that moment that something is not right. He tenses. Looks serious. His face changes. He doesn't look as happy to see me anymore. I look at him while I wait for him to respond. To one of my questions. To any of the million questions I have in my head that I haven't asked yet.

Maggie appears in the doorway, just behind John and her father. "Alan?!" her little voice squeaks. Shy and timid, just like she used to be.

"Maggie," I say. I want her to jump in my arms. But she doesn't look happy. Doesn't look excited.

John puts his arm around her and she flinches, just a little. Like she is embarrassed.

And I'm holding flowers like an asshole. While my best friend has his arm around my girl. Not my Maggie, apparently. Not anymore. I don't know what to say. I feel my heart crunch in on itself four times over and break within my chest.

"I see," I say. "Sorry for disturbing you all." I hand the flowers over. "Maggie, these are for you. I told you I'd come back for you. At least I know I tried." I turn my back to the door and start walking to my car. The flush in my face makes me feel like I might faint or throw up or kill John. My ex-best-friend. Fucking traitor.

"Alan!" she calls. And I hear her footsteps behind me.

I turn around but I can't look at her. This is what it must feel like. Heartbreak. It's happening inside me and I can't do anything but take it. I can't look at her. At her sweet face, the betrayal written all over it. The worst feeling I've ever felt delivered by the hands of the girl I love. The girl I waited for. The girl I would have done anything for.

"I didn't think you'd come back," she says. I can hear the guilt in her voice but it doesn't matter now.

"I told you I would," I say.

"We were so young. I didn't think you meant it."

"I always meant it. I thought you knew that."

"I'm sorry."

"Me, too," I say. "I'll always love you, Maggie."

She leans forward and reaches up for my neck and pulls me down into her, squeezing me. Gripping me. Hugging me. I am steel against her melting body. Within moments, I can become rigid. Frozen. Hard. I didn't know that until right now. Neither did she.

I will never love her again.

John comes out into the driveway. And I move Maggie away from me and I swing on him. And then he grabs me and I wrestle him and we are on the ground, punching each other and wrestling each other and Maggie is crying. She wants us to stop. Her father pulls me off John before I really hurt him. I hear him shouting and her crying and John pleading and panting. But my hands and knuckles are bloodied and swollen and things don't look right from this side. The other side of the grass is definitely not greener. The other side of a crossed friendship and a lost love is definitely different. I don't give a shit if it's my birthday or not. I don't care what day it is. Or what town I'm in. Or if I'll make it home in time for dinner like my mom asked.

It's a blur. It's all such a blur. Maggie is looking up at me with tears rolling down her face and John is applying pressure to his nose. Maggie's father is threatening to call the cops on me, I think, if I hear him correctly.

My right eye is swollen and I can hardly see out of it. The flowers I gave Maggie are on the concrete. Blood is all around me.

Maggie is still beautiful when she cries, but it isn't the same kind of beautiful I thought she was before.

THIRTY-FOUR

I WAKE up to the sound of screaming. Someone. Mom? I jump out of bed and run to where the noise is coming from. No. I realize it's my aunt screaming when I make it to my mother's bedroom. Where my aunt is hovering over my mom, shaking her body, screaming. Over and over she's screaming. Screaming for her to wake up. Screaming for me to call help. Screaming for me to get out of there. Screaming that I shouldn't look. That I shouldn't see my mother this way. Screaming that she isn't breathing. Screaming that something is wrong.

And then she's screaming, "Oh, god, I think she's dead!"

I am in the kitchen now, dialing 911. My heart is beating faster than I can keep track of. I wonder if she's dead. If I'm about to die, too. If this is real. If any of this is fucking real. The operator answers the phone.

"911, what's your emergency?" Her voice is calm, too calm. Too pleasant. Too light. This is not matching up.

I have tears welling in my eyes before I can speak. Before I think I could ever say these words out loud. I'm afraid if I say the words and she's not dead, then the words will kill her. I'm afraid if I say the words, they will be true. I'm afraid if I say the words...

"Hello, 911, what's your emergency?" she repeats.

I clear my throat and I try to form a sentence. "My mom, there's something wrong. Please send someone right now. Please." I can't bring myself to say it out loud. That she might be dead. She asks me for the address and everything is blank. Everything is cold. Everything is a blur. I feel like I am leaving my body as I tell her the address.

"Is she breathing?" she asks.

"I, I don't know. I don't know." I must repeat it over and over until she finally tells me to calm down. But I thought I was calm? Calmer outside than I feel inside where everything feels like it's shutting down.

She asks me what happened. I am again saying I don't know. And I wonder how many times I have to say I don't know for her to understand that I don't fucking know. That I have no idea what is happening right now. That I went to bed and my mother was alive and then I woke up and she might not be anymore. That I feel like I woke up in some parallel universe where my mother might be gone.

She says an ambulance and squad are on the way. She says to stay calm. She asks if I know how to do CPR. I walk like a person with no direction in life, a zombie, a numbed patient, to my mother's bedroom. My aunt is kneeling beside the bed, clutching my mother's unmoving hand, her face looking down. I hear her sobs, even though they are much quieter now. I tap her on the shoulder and hand her the phone.

She lets go of my mother's hand and takes the phone. She wipes her eyes and puts the phone to her ear. "Hello?" she asks, her voice not cracking. She walks out of the room, and I hear her voice echo like a rumbling train in the distance.

My mother's dark hair is staining the pillow. Her eyes are closed. No shadow of a smile paints her lips. From here, she looks like she's just sleeping, dreaming a dream that does not move her. I walk over to the side of the bed where her face is looking, where my aunt was just kneeling. And I drop down and take her hand in mine. It's not cold. I put my finger to her nose to see if any warm breath touches me. It doesn't come.

"Come on, Mom. Breathe," I whisper, without thinking. It just comes out. There is no answer. No breath. No life.

It is a strange thing to kneel beside your mother's bed – the woman who brought you here, the woman who took care of you, the woman who raised you – and know that she is here, but she is not. To know that she is gone. And it is an empty, disastrous thing to see the woman who gave you life with none of her own. There is nothing that can prepare you for this. Tears start to fill my eyes, sadness and anger taking over my body. I know I will be unable to control what happens next. What human response I might have. I have to look away then.

My heart is pounding and my eyes are burning and my mother is dead? I can't breathe. I feel like someone stole the life right from my chest. The ability to think. To feel. My eyes travel over to the nightstand – there is an almost-empty glass of what is definitely vodka and orange juice, and a liter of Traveler's Club vodka that is still 1/3 full. I should have tried harder to get her to stop drinking. I should have been a better son. I should have made her feel more loved, while my dad was still here and even more after he left. My eyes fall to the floor. A bottle of pills. I pick it up. It's empty. It's empty? I look at the name on the prescription and it does not belong to my mother. It is my aunt's name on the label. Alprazolam. Xanax.

I look at my mother's drink again. I smell it. Definitely orange juice and vodka. Something is wrong. My mother always finishes her drink. Always. And no matter how drunk she is, she puts away the liquor bottle so no one can see it.

My aunt comes back in the room and says the ambulance should be here any minute.

"I think she killed herself," I say.

"What? She would never..."

"Look." I hold up the empty bottle of pills. "Don't say she wouldn't when she just did." I look at the nightstand and I know if she meant to die, she'd let me know. She'd tell me. My mother is not a selfish woman. I look at her face again, she has makeup on. I think she meant to do this. She always washes her face before bed. I pick up the bottle and nothing is under it. I pick up the cup. I look behind the nightstand. Under it. Under the bed. Nothing. I open the nightstand drawer. Nothing is in there but random crap. I stand up and I look around. I hear the ambulance and police outside. A knock on the door.

My eyes scan the room and I see the dresser. Nothing is on top of it. But my aunt sees me looking, searching.

She starts shaking and sobbing. "No, Alan, don't tell me she did this on purpose." She stays where she is.

My hands are shaking as I search through drawers, through the closet. But I stop. There are no notes. My mother was a private person and we will both respect that even now, even though she is gone. Even though secrets don't mean a fucking thing anymore.

I leave the room as the squad is banging on the door. But I don't go to the door. I go to my room, and I close the door behind me. And I walk over to my bed and sit on it. My hands are still shaking. Still shaking. And I am asking whatever is out there, why this is happening. Why my mother felt the need to end her own life. Why she left me. Why. Why?

Tears are falling from my eyes for all the things I wish I could say to her right now. I run into my mother's room where they are checking her, saying things, counting things. I run over to her and throw my body on hers. Because I just can't accept that this is the last time I will ever see her again. And I cry into her hair and I hug her. "I love you, Mom. I'm so sorry. I'm so sorry. I'm so sorry I couldn't be a better son. I will miss you more than you'll ever know."

She is pronounced dead just moments after that.

I am still 18 years old and still nursing a broken heart when it breaks all over again, in a different way. In a way I'm afraid I will never recover from.

THIRTY-FIVE

IT IS April 8th and I'm wondering if my mother's suicide had anything to do with her miscarriage. Or the fact that my dad left. Or maybe both. Maybe me, too. Maybe all of it. Maybe all of us. Maybe the whole picture.

I have so many questions that will never be answered. I am packing up her belongings. Her clothes, for goodwill. Her pictures, for me. There are photos from before I was born. My aunt takes most of those. Except a few that I want.

The one of my mother in her 70's outfit, glowing like a little hippie with braids outside of some peace bus. I wanted that one. I keep it. I save it. The one of my mother, pregnant with me. Her belly is so big for her tiny frame. She's smiling, really smiling. A real smile with clear eyes and an expression I hardly remember ever seeing her wear.

A photo of her in the hospital, holding me. Little tiny newborn me. With a red face and closed eyes and no fucking idea that I am alive. Her, exhausted but so happy. Her hospital gown on. Her, under the sheets in that hospital bed.

In the delivery room. Looking down at me, smiling. No makeup. No facade. No bottle. Just happy.

My father, sleeping in the chair in the room as she's glowing like a new mother would. And I wonder if I was a burden to her then. And if I was, why does she look so happy about it? My aunt is in the next picture, holding balloons and flowers at first, as she entered the room. In the next, my aunt is holding me. At first, my mother is watching, smiling. In the next photo, she is sleeping. My father is holding me.

I look at the image and I try to remember a time where he ever looked this sensitive or kind in reality. I can't. So I stop trying.

The next batch of photos are so plentiful. It seems like every waking moment of my first year of life. Every smile, every grin, every funny face, every time I cried. Then it is a picture of my mother with her hands on her belly, like she's expecting again. I'm on the carpet next to her feet, looking up at her.

Then there are a few ultrasound pictures. *Alyssa.* My little sister, I assume. Then the pictures mostly stop, except for a few random ones that other people had taken. Like my aunt. Or my friends. Or my school. Or my dad's family.

And in none of the pictures after that does my mother ever look happy again.

I walk out of the room and into the living room where my aunt is making phone calls and waiting for food to finish cooking and doing anything really to pass the time. Her sister is dead. My mother. The person who connected us is no longer here and I feel the urge to flee. I am no longer welcome here. I know it. She knows it. Or at least, I feel like she knows it. I am a stranger here, now. A charity case. But I am an adult. I am 18. I need to leave. I don't need a foster home and she is not my guardian and I am not her responsibility.

"Did you know?" I ask, interrupting her doing nothing.

She turns to look at me. Her eyes are swollen. "Know what?" she asks.

"About Alyssa." I toss the picture to her. Of my mother with her hands on her belly.

She swallows then. It is uncomfortable. We're both uncomfortable. She picks up the photo from the floor. "Her little girl. She said I might not understand you, but I'd understand her."

She starts sobbing. Then she throws her face in her hands. "You just looked so much like your father. I didn't understand why she'd want a baby with him. Why she'd want to have kids with him. She said I wouldn't understand. She was right. I didn't. I wouldn't. I couldn't. Your father was such a terrible person most of the time. When our mom died, your mom took care of me. I was the older one. I was supposed to do that. I didn't have it in me. Your mom did. She did.

She met your dad, she got pregnant. She had you. I told her not to. I told her to leave him. She wouldn't give you up. It was you, not him, she was fighting for. When she lost your sister, god, it was all over after that. She lost it. Something snapped. She became everything she hated. And she hated everything after that. I should have done more. I should have been there." She is punching the carpet now. Angry, and regretful. And sad. And mad. Every emotion possible.

I am watching from a safe distance even though I feel like I should go hug her. But instead I let her cry. Because sometimes, people just need to cry. When she pulls herself together, I go over to her. I put my arm over her shoulder, and then I hug her.

"You were a good sister, and a good aunt," I say, trying to make her feel less shitty. "Mom really loved you. So much."

"I know she did," she says.

"Alyssa?" I ask. "What happened with my sister? I never even knew I would have had a sister until Mom told me one night when she was wasted."

"Your father beat her when she was pregnant. She lost the baby. She was never the same after that."

I can feel my face contort into something unimaginable. Something hard. Something angry. When I don't answer, she speaks again.

"You were only about a year old. You wouldn't have known."

I wouldn't have if she hadn't told me. But she did. And I didn't know if my mom even remembered. It didn't matter now though. Alyssa was gone. My mom is gone now, too.

And my dad? Who knows where the fuck he is?

"Does my dad know?" I finally ask.

She swallows and avoids the question.

"Does my dad know that my mother is dead?" I ask.

She shakes her head in silence. "I have his phone number and new address. If you want it."

I just nod. "Yeah, take your time though. I'm not in a rush to contact him."

She doesn't look at me when she says "okay" and then busies herself with something else, something away from this topic.

I don't blame her. It's a sore subject. For both of us. I don't know when the last time she saw him was. I haven't seen him since the night my mom kicked him out. I haven't spoken to him. I have had no contact with him and I haven't cared. Until now.

Until I know the real reason why my mother lost my baby sister. Until I know what made him think it was okay to beat his pregnant wife. Until he knows how truly depressed it made my mother. Until he knows just how much destruction he left in his path with the heel of his boot and the palm of his hand.

Until I accept the fact that my mother just killed herself, and he is mostly to blame. Even though I realize that this damage is irreversible. Even though I know, knowing anything won't change anything. Even though I realize no answers will bring her back.

THIRTY-SIX

IT HAS BEEN a week since my mom died and it still seems like nothing is real anymore. People, places, things. They all seem hollow, empty, made of plastic, or worse, something I can't even touch. Something I can't even hold before it disappears. I am just, going, at this point. One foot in front of the other. Moving forward. Pushing on against the current. Because it's the only choice I have. I could break down and crumble and waste away, but life will keep going. It will move on with or without me. With or without my mother. So I do what I can.

I pull myself together every morning and get dressed and button on a smile. I put one leg in my jeans at a time. One shoe on first, then the other. A shirt. It's warm. But sometimes I put on a sweatshirt just because I'm so uncomfortable that at least if it's physical I can blame the unsettling, itchy factor on that. *It's the sweatshirt. It's 80 degrees. It's the sweatshirt.*

It's not the fact that my mother is dead and I'm alone in the world now. Maybe I always have been, even when she was here. No. We had each other despite the miles between us even when she was standing right next to me. No. It's the sweatshirt. I wash my hands so often these days that they're dry and irritated all the time, which only makes me want to wash them more.

Today I open my closet and pull out my one good suit. I wish it wasn't black. I wish it wasn't so dark. So somber and sad. Maybe I just wish I didn't have to wear it for this occasion.

"Alan?"

I hear my aunt call me from the living room.

"Yeah," I yell back.

"Almost ready?"

I button up my shirt and put my tie on and straighten it. I look at myself in the mirror. My dark hair is freshly cut since I went to the barber yesterday. My brown eyes are looking back at me, not as happy as I swore they were. I look sad. But in this suit, I look grown. I don't recognize the man staring back at me. I feel like I was just a boy yesterday. Well, maybe not yesterday. I had to grow up fast. But this man standing in front of me, he looks like a stranger. I don't remember being this tall. This heavy. This tired. My shoulders are broad and in this light I look like my father. A younger version of him. Even the way I stand reminds me of him. The face I'm making. I hate it. And I hate myself, too.

I take one last look at myself and smooth my jacket. I'm ready, but I won't say it. I'll just go out there to meet her. I take seven wide steps before I'm out of my bedroom and into the entryway of the living room. My aunt is wearing a black dress. Knee-length. Her usually unruly hair has been straightened and she's wearing makeup that makes her look pretty. But she's pretty in a sad way. And her heels don't look comfortable.

"You look so handsome, Al," she says, with a small attempt at a smile.

And I know she's thinking she wishes my mother could be here.

"You really grew up," she says. "You don't look like a little boy anymore."

I nod and shift where I stand. "I'll drive."

She grabs the urn with my mother's ashes in them. "I wish more people could come," she says. "But, your mother would have wanted it to be just us."

I nod again. "She was always a pretty private person."

"That she was," she says. She grabs the dozen blue balloons she got from the dollar store and looks at them. "One time she told me that if she ever died, she wanted blue balloons for her memorial and her ashes spread in the water. Not sure why she wanted blue though. Pink was always her favorite color."

But I smile. And it isn't a sad smile. I know why she wanted blue. And for a second, I think I want to cry, because she really did love me. Even if I thought she didn't. I hold the door for my aunt as she walks out and I take the urn for her.

Once we're in the car, we head to the lake where my mother wanted us to spread her ashes. Said she always loved the water. Always wanted to be free. To float. To drift. To be a part of something clear and beautiful and moving. To be a part of something people might look at and feel peace.

When we get to the lake, I open the car door for my aunt, who is already starting to tear up. She puts her sunglasses on. Maybe because it's sunny out. Or maybe it's because she doesn't want me to see her cry. Either way, I don't ask. We walk the path to the edge of the water. To the exact place my mother specifically requested we throw her ashes.

My aunt hands me the balloons and pulls out her piece of paper first. She wrote something. So did I.

She clears her throat and wipes her eye under her sunglasses. "Dee, from the moment you were born I knew you were going to be a pain in my ass. But I also knew you were going to be the most important person in my life. My baby sister. My best friend." Her voice catches and cracks on the last two words. She swallows and her tone is shakier when she speaks again. "It was my job to protect you. To take care of you. To teach you. But you did those things for me. I learned more from you than our own parents. I learned more from you than anyone else in my entire life. You taught me what it meant to love someone more than you love yourself. I wish I could have protected you. But I failed you. And I will always be sorry for that.

Still, if you were here, you'd tell me to shut up. That if I blamed myself again, you'd slap me. So instead, I'll do what you asked. I will remember the good times and always think of you in the light you asked me to. In the memories that were good. In the forts we used to make growing up. In the pink nail polish we'd paint on each other's nails. In the secrets we whispered to each other about boys. In the tears we cried when they broke our hearts. In the delivery room when your baby boy was born. It was then that I watched you become a mother. The best mother a kid could ever ask for."

My eyes well up and I swallow down the tears.

She takes a moment and removes her sunglasses and wipes her eyes with a tissue. She sobs into the tissue for a minute. "I love you, Dee. Just know that you were the best sister I could have ever had."

She opens the urn and pulls out some of her ashes with her hand, then sprinkles them into the water. "I hope wherever you are, you're happy."

My eyes are burning and I'm blinking so I don't cry. I know it's my turn. I hand her the balloons and she hands me the urn.

She nods and puts her sunglasses back on, holding the balloon strings to her chest.

I pull my piece of paper from my pocket and open it up. When I wrote it, I didn't know what to say. I wrote it so many times and crumpled up so many pieces of paper that found their way to the trashcan that I stopped counting.

I look down at the paper and start to read, trying to keep my voice even. "Mom, we weren't always close but that didn't make it feel like we weren't. You were the one person I knew I could always count on. The one person I knew would be there for me. The one person I knew I could tell anything to without feeling like an idiot. The one person I knew would care about me no matter what. I'm sorry I didn't try to talk to you more, and I'm sorry you didn't try to talk to me more. I wish we could have gotten to know each other better. I thought we'd have time for that. Later. When I grew up. When I became a man. Or when you became sober. I'm sorry if I ruined your life. I never meant to. I tried not to get in your way. I tried to be a good kid for you. I know you said you wish you could have been a better mother. Well, I wish I could have been a better son. Maybe in the next life, we'll find that we were the best mother and son that each of us could be at the time. I love you. Now. Then. And always."

My aunt is sobbing as I fold the piece of paper and stick it back into my pocket. I open the urn and stick my hand in and just the thought of pulling out my mother's ashes disturbs me. But this is what she wants. So I walk over to the edge of the water and I stick my hand in and pull out some of her remains. I toss them into the water, sprinkling them as gently as I can. "I love you, Mom. You're free now. Kiss Alyssa for me."

I watch the ashes as they fly away in the breeze, hoping they land in the water. I hear my aunt crying behind me. And I put the top back on the urn and turn to look at her. "Here," I say to her, holding out my hand, requesting the balloons.

She hands them to me. And I separate them. I hand her back six. And I'm holding six balloon strings in my left hand, with the urn in my right. And I look up at the blue balloons and that's when my first tear falls. I look at my aunt. "Ready?"

She nods, but her face is twisted. It's too painful for her. Too painful for us both. For different reasons. We let them go, at the same time. And we both look up and watch the blue balloons float up into the clear sky.

As the balloons fade from my sight, I feel my heart break inside my chest. It breaks in such a way that I don't know how to start picking up the pieces. And as my heart is breaking, I want the one person who could hold me and tell me it would be okay without making me feel ashamed about crying. But she's gone.

And I know why she wanted blue. She wanted blue for me. Her final way of telling me how much she loved me.

THIRTY-SEVEN

I WAKE up in my new apartment and I realize there is no one to check on. I live alone now. My mom is dead. My aunt is at her house. This happens almost every day. I don't need to listen out for screams or cries for help. It's just me in here.

The room is dark and it smells like paint. The apartment was just renovated before I got here. My bed is empty and I hate when it's empty. I roll over to face the clock. 2:53am. I guess she left before I could ask her to stay.

Meeting girls at bars doesn't really hold much promise. They meet you, want to fuck you, come home with you and do just that, and sometimes – like tonight – they split. Before you wake up. Before you can make them breakfast.

I remember my night with her. I met her at the bar. She smiled at me. I walked up to her. She tossed her hair over her shoulder. Touched my arm. Whispered into my ear because I couldn't hear her over the music. I asked her where she was headed afterwards. If she wanted to come back to my place.

We arrived here in a tumble of kisses and want. Her arms around me, mine around her. Picking her up on the way in and closing the door behind us. I carried her upstairs to my bedroom where she was practically begging me to take her clothes off. So I did. She didn't have to beg.

I started with her lips. Then her breasts. Her hips. I kissed every inch of her and worshipped her beautiful body like it was the last time I'd ever see it. And fuck, she responded. She came twice, and after, she gripped on to my shoulders like she'd never been treated like this before. I thought for a second she was going to tell me she loved me. But I didn't know if she even remembered my name.

Apparently, she didn't. I turn on the light on the nightstand and I look at my empty bed. Sometimes I miss hearing things in the night. Someone crying. Someone screaming. Someone needing me. Here, it's just me. You don't know what it feels like to be alone, utterly and truly alone, until you do. Waking up in an empty bed in an empty apartment and I wish I could get a dog but the complex won't allow it.

Barking. They'll bark. They'll make noise. They might be dangerous. Might ruin the floors. Dogs might ruin the floors but people ruin homes. They ruin entire lives. Meanwhile, they don't say anything on the lease about strangers coming and going into your apartment at all hours of the night. Isn't that more dangerous? Fuck, what was that girl's name? Amber?

She had strawberry blonde hair and legs for days. She smiled at me from across the bar. I'm not 21, but I get in anyway. Probably because I'm so tall and because I look older than I am. I look aged, not like a fine wine or any of that bullshit. Just, aged. Tired. Old. I've seen enough shit to make me look that way.

It's been three months since I said goodbye to my mom. And it's been one month since I've moved in here. There have been six women to come and go since then. Six women in one month. I think at this rate I may run out of women in this town. I wake up and I go in to the kitchen and wash my hands.

It's 3am and I can't sleep and I wish Amber was like the last one. I wish she stayed. Spent the night with me. I like having warm hands wrap around me making me feel wanted, making me feel at least a little safe. But it isn't just about that.

Lately, I just want to feel good. The warmth of a woman does that for me. Makes me feel good. Makes me feel wanted. Makes me feel something. Anything.

I don't know if I want them to stay and they don't ever know if they want to either. Every night is a coin toss. A should I or shouldn't I? A will he or won't he? A yes, maybe, or no. I like not knowing what the end will feel like. I like guessing. I like the drama of the anticipation. I like the taste of the pull, the tug. The game. It's exciting. It's distracting. It's depressing.

I just want to feel good. And these girls, apparently they want to feel good, too. I get up and I wash my hands and get a water bottle from the fridge. I drink it. I wonder if Amber remembers my name. I wonder if she cared what it was in the first place. I try to remember if she asked me what it was. If she ever even asked me for my name.

But it doesn't matter. I fulfilled whatever it was that she wanted or needed. And I guess she did the same for me. At least temporarily. I just wish she was here so I could appreciate her all over again.

Amber. What a pretty name. What a pretty girl. What a pretty pussy. What a pretty ugly way to end the night, thinking of the girl you had, the girl you almost had, if she didn't saunter out of your bed in the middle of the night while you were sleeping. The girl who wanted you, but not enough to stay. Not enough to really look at you. But it's okay, because I guess I didn't really look at her either. What color were her eyes? What did she say she did for work? Fuck it. Who cares?

At the end of the day it was obvious. Neither of us really cared. If we did, we wouldn't have fucked each other like two strangers who met at a bar who would probably never see each other again. We wouldn't have kissed each other like it was the last time we ever would. Maybe it wouldn't have been as good if we did anything differently. Maybe we would have never gone home with each other in the first place if we were looking for someone to really get attached to. And maybe that was on purpose.

Maybe it was easier to fuck people and forget them, instead of getting to know them and doing something stupid – like falling in love.

THIRTY-EIGHT

I AM 21 years old now. I've started frequenting several bars. Too often. I've been in this apartment for about three years now and I'm starting to wonder if I should start thinking about leaving this town, too. Shitty suburban areas in New Jersey don't seem like they're meant for me. One of my biggest fears is living and dying in the same state I grew up in. But at least I'm not in the same town I was raised in. Just the same state.

Jersey has a way of wrapping its arms around you and making it feel like it's the only state for you. Like you're safe here. Like it's your home. Like there is no other state out there. And in a way, there isn't. At least not for me. Seems like most people don't leave Jersey and why would they? We have the city so close to us. The place where dreams come true, supposedly. But really, the prices in Jersey are high enough. We don't stray there to live unless we can afford it, and most of us can't.

I've been working construction through a guy I know.

The pay is good. I make enough to make rent and drink and smoke on the side. Life is pretty good. I've got more women than I know what to do with most of the time. Sometimes, it feels like it still isn't enough. And that scares me.

Sometimes – okay, a lot of times – I just like to get fucked up. Fucked up to the point of not feeling whatever it is that was left inside me when my mom died. There's really nothing to look forward to, except women. They're the only thing that keeps me going most days, like today.

I'm sitting in a bar I've been in far too many times. I know all the bartenders by name at this point. I call Stacy over and can't keep myself from flirting with her. She's stunning. Long black hair, tattoos. Killer smile. But I can't fuck her. I can't shit where I eat. But if she wanted to, I'm sure I wouldn't say no. I can't imagine anyone saying no to that girl. I tip her well every time I come. Sometimes I wonder if she pays part of her rent just with my tips alone. I go to different bars because if you go to the same one long enough, the crowd is always the same. Which means the girls start to become the same. Which means chances are you've taken quite a few of them home. At least that's how it goes for me.

Tonight there are some girls who came from about an hour away. They heard the fried pickles were good here. And I don't disagree when they ask me my opinion.

Tonight I've got my eye on Liz, a tall brunette from out of town. She's laying the flirting down heavy and made it clear she likes my face. She said it, more than once. A bona fide green light. When she asks me if I live nearby, I tell her I'm four miles away. And I've got room if her girlfriends want to crash. I tell her I'd be glad to drive them back in the morning if they feel like giving their designated driver a break. They love that. Of course, it comes after a slight hesitation. But with the other girls drinking, they're all down to take the party back to my place. I tell them I have a couch and a king-size bed, but it doesn't take much convincing.

Liz is all for it. She's touching my arm every time she talks to me. A glint in her eye that tells me she wants the bed, with me in it.

I tell them to save their money on drinks. I've got plenty at the apartment. And I drive us all back to my place.

When I pull my car into the driveway, they're halfway between tired and full on party mode. Liz sits up front with me, of course. Her hand is on my leg the whole way. We get out of the car and I unlock the door and let them all in first. One, two, three beautiful girls, entering my apartment like pretty little ducklings. I tell them there are drinks in the kitchen and to make themselves at home.

Liz finds the radio in the kitchen and turns it up as her girlfriend starts pouring shots for everyone. They're all dancing now and I just laugh. This is what I think I love most about women. Their ability to turn any house into a home. Their way of bringing fun and ease and comfort to a place that doesn't have a shred of it. The way they lighten a room and make you smile. Girls, there's nothing fucking better. For a second I want to keep them. Ask them all if they just want to move right in right now. It can be like this every day, I'd tell them. In all the three years I've lived here, my apartment has never been so alive. It has never felt so much like a home and so much less like a crypt. And then I realize these girls, dancing, they don't know they're practicing necromancy right where they stand. Right beneath their pretty little feet. And I don't realize I'm smiling when they ask me if I want a shot.

Of course I do. We party and drink and I'm happy. They're happy. And when it's time to go to sleep, I offer the bed to all of them but Liz smacks me and says "No". She directs Crystal and Lourdes to the couch and pulls me by my hand to my room. I'm laughing at her firmness. At her lack of being discreet.

When we get into the room she kisses me for the first time. I don't know what time it is but I know it's late. I'd be sleeping already if it weren't for them. But tomorrow is Saturday and I don't care how late we stay up. Tonight is about her. And I kiss her back, and something weird is happening. I think I like her.

The sex is amazing. It's soft, and slow at first. We take our time before we finish and nothing is hurried about it until we're both close. And I think she likes me, too. Afterwards, we cuddle. A close cuddle, a sort of sleeping together that has an intimacy I don't usually feel. And when we wake up, I don't want her to leave. I tell her I would offer to make them breakfast but I don't have anything. So I go pick up bagels for them, and Liz comes with me. They don't leave until around noon. Before they go, Liz pulls on my shirt.

"Take my phone number. I want to see you again," she says.

"I want to see you again, too," I say. And I take her number.

And I drive them back to the bar. Her hand is on my leg again, the whole way. I don't tell her to stop but I don't really flirt back. I never do. Part of the reason is because I don't know what to say. I don't have that type of personality. The gimmicks. The jokes. The knight in shining armor thing. I'm just a guy looking for someone to keep me company for a little while. A guy looking for a girl to make me not feel as alone I do. It's usually it's comes in the form of sex. It just happens. And then it's over. And she leaves.

Just like Liz does. We date for two weeks of solid heaven before I get drunk and cheat on her with a girl whose name I don't even know. We almost fall in love before she starts to hate me. Almost.

THIRTY-NINE

I WAKE up and I'm 24. I spent my birthday yesterday drunk at home by myself and passed out on the couch. It's been eight years since I've seen or spoken to my father but I still have his number and address that my aunt gave me. I don't know why, but I held on to it. Maybe because I knew someday I'd want to call him. Maybe because I knew someday I might want to visit him. Talk to him, man to man. I couldn't have closure with my mom but I could still have it with him. Or something that resembles closure, anyway. Something to soften the anger. If anything can, I need to try it.

I walk to my bedroom and pull out the number and address that I've kept in the drawer of my nightstand. I stare at his name. Brent Shaden. Just seeing his name fills me with a boiling rage. Just knowing I'm going to call him pisses me off. In all these years, he never called to see how I was. To wish me a happy birthday. To check in. I don't even know if he knows my mom is dead. And worse, I don't know if he even cares.

I take out my cell phone, a cheap shitty flip phone, and I call his number. It's ringing. I don't know if I expect him to answer or not and I don't know which would be worse, but my heart is pounding. I get his voicemail. The no-personality, informal voicemail that just has him saying his name – "Brent Shaden" – and it beeps.

"It's your son, Alan. Call me back," I say. I click the button to end the call and my hands are shaking.

Three hours and twenty-one minutes pass and I think that's it. The piece of shit isn't even going to call me back. But my phone rings. And it's him.

"Hello?" I say, because I don't know where else to start.

"Alan, it's Dad," he says. "It's so good to hear your voice, son."

Bullshit. Every word is bullshit. But I say, "It is?"

"Of course it is. I've been wanting to reach out to you, just didn't think you wanted to hear from me. God, how old are you now? 23? 24?"

"24. My birthday was yesterday."

"That's right. These days mess me up anymore. Can't keep dates straight with old age, you know?"

"Yeah, sure."

"How are you, son? How's your mom doing?"

And it hits me that he doesn't know. Has no idea. "Mom died."

I hear an audible gasp, a convincing sound to let me know this news just hit him like a train. Then a pause.

His voice is different when he speaks again. More authentic. Concerned. "What? When?"

"Six years ago, this February," I say.

"How?"

"I'm pretty sure she killed herself."

"She what?" He makes a noise. I don't know if it's a cough, a quiet cry. I don't know what it is but it's repulsive.

I want to tell him it was because of him, just to hurt him. But I don't. I know enough to know I can't blame him for everything. I know that he wasn't the one who forced the pills down her throat. I know we are all accountable for our own decisions. But I know I don't have to say it, because I know he feels the weight of this. We both know he played a role, no matter how major or minor. And he has to live with that.

His voice is thick now, raised, and full of the father I used to know. "God damn it, why didn't you call me? Why didn't anyone call me?"

I flinch. But I raise my voice to match his. "Why didn't you fucking call us?" Silence. "Look, I don't want to fight. That's not why I called. I want to come see you. I think we should talk before you die, too."

"Yeah," he says. "Okay. Let's do that."

He asks if I'm still in Jersey. I tell him yes. He tells me he's in Florida now, moved there after he left Mom, and gives me the same address that's written on the paper. I tell him I'll drive down this weekend.

The drive is about 22 hours and I leave Friday after work. I'd have gotten a plane ticket, but I don't think either of us want to spend an entire weekend together. Shit, I don't think either of us want to spend a day together. I figure I'll stop at a hotel about halfway between Jersey and Florida, and that's exactly what I do. I pit stop in Raleigh, North Carolina. I'm not halfway but I'm tired, and I just physically can't drive anymore. Or don't want to, rather. I get a hotel room and get back on the road five hours later.

I get to my father's house at 7:18pm. I pull in a driveway that belongs to a small, weathered looking home. My dad always worked construction, using his hands. I'm surprised the gutters and siding are in as bad of a shape as they are.

I get out of my car and walk up the driveway. It's warm here. Humid. Hotter than Jersey. I walk to the front door and have no idea what's going to happen. For a second, I wonder if this will result in one or both of us bleeding. I remember the way he used to beat my ass and wonder if he'd dare try to hit me today. I ring the doorbell anyway. I'm not wearing a belt. I didn't bring one. I don't need one to hurt him.

The man who opens the door is not the same scary man I remember. He's aged. Boy, has he aged. His hair is completely gray, no dark specks to remind me of the man he was when I last saw him. His face is worn, weathered from time just like the house. In his gray t-shirt and jeans, he still looks like he's in pretty good shape. But, this man is older. Weaker.

His expression changes from surprised to happy to angry to neutral. Blank. He looks at me like I'm not the same kid he used to know. And I'm not. I straighten my shoulders and face as he looks at me.

"Alan," he says, unsure what to do. "Care to give your old man a hug?"

I swallow. But I hug him. His arms are already outstretched and waiting and for some reason, there's still some small part of me that doesn't want to disappoint him. Though I could never figure out why.

"Come in," he says, holding the door for me.

"Thanks," I say, walking in. I look around. It's definitely not decorated like Mom would have it. Or like any woman would have it. And for a second I think our homes are kind of similar. Empty, plain. No sign of female life. No sign of much life at all.

I ask him if I can have a drink and open the fridge. It's mostly empty, just like mine. There's milk and beer. And I pop open two beers with my lighter and hand him one.

"Thanks, Al. Cheers. It's been too long," he says, clinking his Heineken to mine.

I let him tap my beer with his and try to smile. Silence. I don't speak because I don't know where to start. He offers.

"Want to go out back and have a smoke? Got a nice view of the canal out there."

"Sure. Let's see it."

He starts walking and I follow. "How long you been living out here?" I ask, to pass the time.

"Since I left," he says. "I came out here and stayed in a hotel until I found this house. Put an offer in and moved in pretty quick. I just needed something small, but with an extra room in case, you know."

"In case what?"

"In case your mom wanted me back. In case you two came out. Got an extra bedroom for you in case you ever needed it."

I take a big swig of the beer and finish about half of it right then, surprised he'd ever take me into consideration.

I look out at the canal. At the dirty swamp water. Wondering what to say to the only parent I have left. To the parent I haven't seen in eight years. To the parent who, only just now, I realize might actually love me. In his own fucked up way.

FORTY

THE SUN IS GLISTENING off the swamp when he speaks again, when the air is filled with something other than this strange silence.

"I'm sorry about your mother. And that I wasn't there."

I don't turn to look at him because I'm afraid to see any sort of false sincerity. Because I will hit him. I just take a drink of my beer and nod. I don't say I'm sorry, because I'm not. I'm not sorry he wasn't there.

"I love you, you know. And I loved your mom."

That's when I turn to look at him. At his mention of the word. "Love?" I ask. "Is that what you call it?" I can feel my face hardening into something I wouldn't recognize if I saw it in the mirror.

He looks back at me for a few moments before he looks away and chugs his beer. "I did the best I could."

I let out a small laugh. "Well, shit. If that was your best I'd hate to see what your worst looks like."

"You know, if you have something to say to me, then you oughta say it right now," he says, malice laced in his tone.

I look out at the swamp and take a breath, try to stop myself from breaking his jaw right where he stands. He's too old for me to do that now. Should have done it when I had the chance. But the calm of the water and the lazy tide makes me relax a bit. It's quiet here. Too quiet. Too quiet for me to get loud for no reason. And I turn to him and look him square in the eye, mustering all my courage. Everything I've ever wanted to say to him comes out in six harsh words. "You were a shitty fucking person," I say.

He looks like I've struck him with a heavy object. He looks wounded. Hurt. I expect him to argue, but he doesn't.

"I know," he says, finally. With no defiance. No argument. "I know," he repeats. "I'm sorry."

And when I look away he tries to get me back.

"You're right. I was a shitty fucking person. I'm not that guy anymore. Not that same guy, anyway, you know?"

I don't look at him. I feel a hard lump form in my throat and I swallow it down. My eyes start to blur and all I can think is that I will not cry. Not here. Not today. Not in front of him. I nod and steady myself before I speak again. "And what makes you so different now?"

"Eight years without your family will do that to a man," he says. "I hope you never know what that feels like."

I turn to look at him. To see if he means it. To see if there's any remorse in his eyes. Regret. Anything resembling honesty.

He's standing near the edge of the water now, looking out at it. Refusing to look at me. I can see in his posture, hand in his pocket, other on his beer, looking down, playing with his one foot on the grass, he's nervous. Fidgety. He doesn't look at me when he says, "Man, Alan, you sure grew up, huh? You're not just a kid anymore. For fuck's sake, you're bigger than I am. How's that for ya? Time, I tell ya, it just passes right on by. If you're lucky, I guess you'd get to notice these things as they start to change. Me, I'm just not that lucky, I guess."

"Luck has nothing to do with it," I say. I finish my beer and go to walk it inside. He follows.

"What's that supposed to mean?" he asks.

"I mean what I said."

"Damn it, Alan. I'm trying here. What do you want me to say, huh? That I was a shit father? A shit husband? I was both, okay. I already said that. What do you want from me? Why'd you come here?"

I open the screen porch and go inside and toss my beer into the recyclable can. Then I turn to look him in the eye. "I want an apology!" I say, but it comes out louder than I expect. "I want you to be sorry and I want you to mean it! All those nights, all those god damn nights, Dad."

He doesn't say anything. He looks ashamed. But I want him to feel this. So I push him. I can't help it. And I keep going. And I push him again. "I want you to be sorry!"

He flinches like it hurts. Not physically. But somewhere else. In a different way. He grabs my arms. "If you put your hands on me again, we're gonna have a problem," he says. His eyes mean business. So does his tone.

But there's something else there. Sadness.

"I never meant to hurt your mother. Or you. I had no idea what the hell I was doing. We didn't plan to have kids. Your mom got pregnant with you and we just guessed as we went. We were young. We were kids ourselves!"

But kids don't get wasted and beat the shit out of their wives. That's what I want to say. But something weird happens when you grow up in a home like this. It's something you don't talk about. Ever. To anyone. Not to each other, not to anyone else. It's all one big warped secret and I'm sick of it. But even here, now, years later when I'm grown and he's old and my mom is dead, it doesn't change. It's still the elephant in the room and no one acknowledges it. No one dares to. Even as I try. It's almost like if you say it out loud then it will all be true. And maybe if you don't, then it won't be. Maybe if you never talk about it, then none of it will have ever happened at all.

I'm tired. Tired from the drive. Tired of the bullshit. Tired from life. I don't say anything. I just look at him.

"Did you come all the way here just to make me feel worse?" he asks. "Because trust me, I have enough regrets for the both of us."

"I don't know why I came here," I say.

"Sure you do," he says. "You want some sort of answer, don't you? But to what? I can't give you an answer if you don't ask the question."

"I guess I just want to know why," I say.

"Why? Why what?"

"Just, why?"

He pauses and looks at me. "You want the long or short answer?" he asks.

"The long one."

"Well, come on then." He walks to the counter and opens a cupboard. Takes out two tumbler glasses and a bottle of Jack. Pours us both a drink. "That'll require something stronger." He hands me the glass and starts walking outside.

I follow him back down to the water's edge. But this time he walks out onto the dock where there's a bench. He sits on it and I sit next to him. It feels strange. Sitting next to my father on this worn bench, after all this time. We sit there like that for a few minutes, drinks in hand, both taking sips in the silence. I start to think he might never speak. For some reason, I feel nervous. Like I'm a kid again in his presence.

"When you asked me 'why' I guess I needed a minute

there. I don't know where to begin. 'Why' is a heavy question, Alan. Sometimes you shouldn't ask questions you don't want to know the answers to. You understand?"

I nod.

"If you're asking why I was a shit father and husband, I don't know. My father raised me, and I guess I turned out to be just like him. If that answers your question. Now if you're asking why that happened, beats the hell out of me. I never wanted to be like him. Not really. Not in certain ways. But he was my dad, kids always look up to their dads, don't they? I guess sometimes we become just like them even if we don't want to. Life is strange like that. Sometimes you become the very thing that you hate. Sometimes it's all you know."

I look out at the water and sit there. I don't say anything. I don't know what to say. My father became his father and I hope I don't become mine.

"You remember your grandpa? My pops?" he asks.

"Vaguely," I say. "I remember you guys teaching me how to play baseball in the backyard."

He laughs. "Yeah, he was a sports guy. Made me like 'em even though I didn't."

"I remember his wake."

He swallows and his posture changes. "Yeah. I remember that, too. How could I forget? Cancer's a hell of a bitch. Didn't even look like himself when he went."

I nod. And I try to remember when my grandpa died. I try to remember if I even hugged my father or said I was sorry. I don't think I did. I don't remember him ever crying.

"'Why' is such a huge question, Alan. I wish I had a better answer for you. I wish I had any type of answer. Sometimes there is no answer. Sometimes shit just happens. We can try to move forward or we can stay stuck in the past. All I know is feeling sorry for yourself won't get you anywhere."

I nod. "Yeah, you're right."

"You have two options right now. You can hate me, leave here, and never talk to me again. Or you can give me another chance to be your dad and we can try to get to know each other. I'd prefer the latter."

I look at him. And as much as I want to keep hating him, I don't have it in me. A touch of sympathy has hit me somewhere and I almost feel bad for him, looking at his aged and wrinkled face. His gray hair. His sad eyes. I hold out my hand for him to shake, and he does. "It takes a real man to own up to his mistakes, and I appreciate the apology. I'm sorry, too. For never trying to understand you. Until now."

I see tears form in his eyes but he pretends they aren't there. And he brings me in for a hug and pats my back and holds me. I consider bringing up the baby, saying her name, watching that crush him. But I don't need to. He knows what he's done. He has to live with that. Not me. And it would only make me just as much of an asshole to rub it in his face. Like he said, it's in the past. Bringing it up now won't change a thing.

We sit there for a few hours, catching up. Talking. I tell him what happened to Mom. I tell him about her service, about the blue balloons. About spreading her ashes. About my apartment, my job. We talk about women. He asks me if I ever want kids, and I tell him I don't think so. He tells me about his job, how he's retiring soon but plans to still work on the side. He tells me one day he will leave this house to me. Says he has an account with money in it that'll be all mine. His only son. And then he brings up a name I haven't heard since I was a kid.

"Hey, you remember that guy Fred I used to work with back in Jersey?"

I feel sick and angry just hearing his name. "Yeah."

"His sister called me last year. Said he died from AIDS. Crazy, huh? You hear about it, but I never actually knew anyone that got it."

"Wow, that is crazy." I feel a wave of nausea rush over me and think I'm actually going to puke on the spot. I tell him I'll be right back, that I have to go to the bathroom. He shouts out directions at me about where it is in the house and I don't hear him. It's just noise. All I can hear is AIDS.

AIDS. AIDS. Fred died from AIDS. Fred. AIDS.

I rush into the bathroom and wash my hands and splash cold water on my face and try to calm down. I look in the mirror. Water is dripping down my face into the white sink that my hands are gripping. I study my face, looking for any sign that I might have AIDS. But I don't know what I'm looking for.

FORTY-ONE

THE NEXT MORNING comes and I cannot stop obsessing over the fact that I probably have AIDS. I think of all the girls I may have given it to. Of all the nights I didn't use protection. I don't scare easily but this is an entirely different level. I wake up in the guest room in my father's home and in this lighting in this strange room, the entire world looks different. I wake up and might have AIDS. I may be dying. I may have infected others. I feel the nausea wash over me again and I'm sweating. The air conditioner is on but I'm fucking sweating. My head feels dizzy. These thoughts are poison. Fred was poison. I hate him more in this moment than I did yesterday and I never thought that was possible.

My father looks like an angel right now in comparison and I find it easier to forgive him. Really forgive him. Not the bullshit kind of forgiveness, but real, genuine forgiveness. I never told him about Fred. I never told anyone. I never will. Shit like that, you don't talk about. I don't have to know what would happen if I told someone about this. They would look at me differently. Maybe even question if I'm gay. For a long time, I thought maybe I was the only one this happened to. I never heard guys talk about stuff like this happening to them. But they should. Whenever I see something on the news, a similar situation to what I went through, it devastates me inside. I know what those little boys went through. It's, not an easy thing for a man to even admit to himself, even after all these years.

I get out of bed and I ask my father if I can use his bathroom to wash up. I take a long hot shower. I am scrubbing my body. Literally scrubbing it. With soap. With my hands. I would wash my skin right off me if I could. Peel back the top layer to look inside. To look for AIDS. See if I can see it. I wonder what it would look like. If there would be deadly alien antibodies swimming in my blood, procreating at this very moment by the thousands.

I scrub more. I start to cry, quietly, violently. I make fists with both hands and I'm shaking. I am cursing to myself. Wishing I never went along with any of it. Wishing. Cursing. Praying. Apologizing. The water mixes with my tears and I wipe my eyes. I want to pound my fist against the wall but I don't want to startle my father. I don't want him to know I'm cursing my entire existence.

I eventually step out of the shower and dry myself with a towel. One look in the mirror shows me that the skin on my arms and chest is bright red from scrubbing. I gently pat myself with the towel and hope it goes away fast. In the guest room, I get dressed in jeans and a t-shirt and put some deodorant on.

I find my father in the kitchen, making coffee for us. He asks if I slept well. I say yes. It's a lie. We chit chat about some bullshit I can't even listen to or be a part of because AIDS could be taking over my body and who gives a shit about the game? I thank him for the coffee. For letting me stay. For a nice time. We promise we'll stay in touch and I tell him he can come stay with me if he ever wants to visit anyone back home.

"It was good seeing you, son. I mean that. Gimme a ring when you get home," he says, pulling me in for a hug.

I hug him back and it isn't forced. For all I know, this is the last time I'll ever see him. I don't know how long someone can live with AIDS but I know I could die from it before we ever get the chance to catch up again. Every moment, I feel like I'm staring death in the eye. Looking down the barrel of a shotgun. There's no way out of this one.

I take 95 North for fucking ever. It never ends. The miles keep coming, keep going. The day turns to night and I'm still driving. I don't even stop this time, except at rest stops – I stop at almost every single one, and wash my hands. Sometimes I piss, in which case, I wash my hands before and after. I drive straight through, down 95 and back to Jersey. All I can think about is scheduling an appointment with my doctor to see if I have AIDS or not. Right now, I don't know what would be worse. Knowing or not knowing. I know I was happier before, before I knew it was a real possibility.

I make it home the next day – Sunday – and I feel like a zombie. My eyes are just about permanently popped open and I swear I can still see the yellow line on the road even though I'm inside, lying on the couch like a bum. I sit there for an hour, thinking I should go to my bed to sleep, but I pass out on the couch.

I wake up later that night, still exhausted, and drag myself into my bedroom where I change into shortts and get into bed. Sleep comes eventually. And then way too soon after that, my alarm wakes me up, screaming in my ear at 5am. I take a shower. At work, I wait until 9am rolls around and I tell the guys I'm going to smoke a cigarette. I walk behind the building we're working at where no one can hear me and I call my primary care doctor. Maria from Dr. Loschiavo's office answers the phone and I ask if there's any way they can fit me in today. I tell her I need to get tested. That someone I have been intimate with has an STD. I tell her I don't know which one, so I want to be tested for everything. I tell her lunchtime works best for me. I can swing by there and still come back to work. She says I really should have a physical when I go. Whatever. I don't care.

"I'll do anything," I say. "Just please, get me in."

"Be here at 12:15pm, honey," she says.

"Thank you so much, Maria. Thank you. I'll see you then."

I tell my boss some bullshit about having to run to the doctor to pay a bill. I don't know why I lie. My boss is cool. I just don't want anyone to know. If it's true. If I do have AIDS. This would be the start of them knowing. I rush over to the doctor's office which is about a half hour from the job site. When I walk in, Maria expects me and greets me with a warm smile.

"Alan, it's so nice to see you," she says, taking out the clip-board with the papers attached. "Just hurry up and fill it out, you know what to do. And hey, calm down. You sounded like you were about to pop a blood vessel on the phone."

I try to smile. "It's just scary," I say.

"I know, baby. You'll be fine. Even if you do have something, there are medications for that stuff. Most of it is curable."

Even for AIDS, Maria? Oh god. I can't tell her. I don't tell her. I smile and nod and say she's right and I fill out the papers. The pen is shaking between my fingers as I put down my insurance information. In case of emergency. I used to always put my mom. Now, I put my aunt's name there even though I never expect her to get a call. I wonder if they'd call her if the results come back and say I do have it.

I give Maria the clipboard back and then I'm sitting, looking around the waiting room. Wondering. Sweating. Nervous. AIDS.

A few minutes later they call my name while I am counting the guests that would not attend my funeral. Ex-girlfriends and past lovers all in there, cursing my name. Some infected, some not. I walk into the room and the girl takes my blood pressure.

She smiles. "White coat syndrome, huh?"

"What?" I ask. It already sounds like she's accusing me of having some sort of disease and we haven't even started.

"Calm down, I'm joking. Your blood pressure is a little high. Must be nervous. Don't be."

Yeah right. That's what I want to tell her. Easy for her to say when she's not the one who may be dying from full blown HIV and AIDS for god knows how long. She says the first thing they need is a urine sample, that the cup is on the counter. Then she says the phlebotomist will be in shortly.

About ten minutes later another woman comes in with gloves on. And tubes. And she tells me I'll only feel a pinch and then I'm watching my blood get sucked out of my body, I'm looking for deformities. Signs. Any evidence in there at all. I want to ask her if she's ever *seen* AIDS but I don't because I don't want her to know. Don't want her to look.

Don't want her to suspect. We finish. She takes the little tubes full of my blood and puts them in her blood tube tray thing and takes it who the fuck knows where. But she leaves and I am alone in here. Always alone. I give the other lady my urine sample when she comes back in and then pay my co-pay to Maria, thank her again, and leave to go back to work.

For five days, I am making lists of all the women I've slept with that I can remember. The ones I used condoms with and the ones I didn't. The ones whose names I don't even remember. Forget about Fred, what if I got something from anyone else? The ones I don't even know if I used protection with. It's a long list. I am evil and I am wondering who will speak at my funeral when I get the phone call on Friday afternoon.

"Hey, Al. Good news. The results came back. Negative," Maria says.

"Negative for what?" I ask.

"For everything. You're good to go."

I hang up the phone and I swing my arm and I'm embarrassed immediately after but I don't care. I don't have AIDS. In fact, by some fucking miracle, I don't have anything at all. I thank god. I look down at my jeans and silently thank my dick. And for the first time in a long time, life feels pretty fucking good.

FORTY-TWO

"SO, ALAN, WHAT BRINGS YOU HERE?" she asks, her tan pantyhose on her legs crossed at the knee. The nameplate on her desk says Selena Torres.

She has a tight pencil skirt on, her legs are showing. I'm looking at her legs. Her thighs beneath that skirt. She has glasses on. Dark frames around her dark eyes. Her dark hair is pulled into a bun and I wonder if she lets it out if it'll be long and curly. This reminds me of a porn I've watched three thousand times and she shouldn't be wearing lipstick. Images flash through my mind of me bending her over that desk. The fantasies start the moment she says my name and I can't last here much longer. I wonder if she'd moan or scream.

"Alan?" she says, her voice light and soft.

"Yeah," I say.

"You do realize you're paying by the hour, right?"

"I thought it was actually only 55 minutes."

She smiles. And it's beautiful. "You're right. And you've already wasted five of them."

"Where do I start?" I ask.

"Wherever you're most comfortable."

"That would be between your legs."

She shifts in her chair and presses her lips together. Uncrosses her legs then crosses the other leg over the opposite side. She scribbles something down and nods. "Okay. And why would that make you most comfortable?"

"The truth?"

She nods. "This is a safe place."

"Because I know you want me there. I know I want to be there. Instead of sitting across from you, unable to touch you."

"Have you ever heard of satyriasis?" she asks, even though she knows I haven't, so she doesn't wait for an answer. "By definition, it's uncontrollable or excessive sexual desire in a man. Would you say this sounds familiar or accurate if you were to look inside your thoughts and be honest with yourself?"

"I think I have a pretty healthy sexual appetite," I say, looking at her legs again.

"But is it healthy?" she asks.

"Very." I smile at her.

Involuntarily, she smiles back and I see the flush of pink in her cheeks. She writes something down then straightens her shoulders. She's trying to stay professional. It's sweet. "What drives your sexual desire?"

"Beautiful women. Like you."

"Do you find your desires to be uncontrollable?"

"Right now, yes."

"What about other times? Is this a daily occurrence?"

"Miss Torres, I'm not that easy. I think you're getting the wrong impression of me."

"Have you ever heard of Sex Addicts Anonymous? I think you should consider going to some meetings in your area. They're absolutely free, completely anonymous, and you could meet others who share your experiences and urges. I've had patients really benefit from the camaraderie of this organization."

"Sex Addicts Anonymous? You think I'm a sex addict?"

"I do. I think most other professionals would agree. If you want, you could always get a second opinion."

I look down for a moment and consider it. I want to wash my hands. Take a shower. This feels wrong. Sitting here, with a therapist, who also happens to be a gorgeous woman, who just labeled me a sex addict like it was no big deal.

"Are you all right?" she asks. "What are you thinking?"

I look up at her. "Do you always change lives this quickly like it's no big deal?"

"You came here for help," she says. "That's all I'm trying to offer."

I nod, slowly. "Okay."

"When did these desires begin? Do you remember?"

"I don't like that question."

She scribbles something down. "Why do you dislike it? Does it make you uncomfortable?"

I nod and start rubbing my hands together. I want to wash them. I need to get clean even though I took a shower before I came here. "How many more minutes do we have left?" I ask.

She looks at her watch. "37."

"Can we just talk? Not about my problems. Or my past. Just, you and me, have a conversation like you're not my therapist and I'm not your patient?"

"That's not proper protocol..."

"Fuck protocol," I say. And I lean forward. "I'm attracted to you. Are you attracted to me?"

She looks at me for a moment and doesn't say anything.

Then she busies herself with the notepad in her hand and starts writing something down.

I stand up and walk over to where she's sitting. I tap my finger on the notepad then hold out my hand for it. She looks up at me and hesitates. She's nervous. "Whatever you're thinking you want to happen, is illegal."

I put the notepad on her desk and go back to my chair. "Do you want me to leave? Because I can't sit here across from you without wanting to touch every inch of you."

"No, it's just, I could lose my license to practice..."

"I'm not your patient anymore. Consider this my last visit. What? Are you afraid I'm gonna get my problems on you? I don't think they're contagious." I grin.

She smiles and groans as I watch her consider this. "Ugh. I've got problems of my own. Lock the door."

I do as she says. Her office is a private suite on the third floor of an office building. I haven't heard a peep coming from anywhere else in the building, so I doubt anyone will hear us. Unless she's a screamer.

I walk back over to her and she's changed now. She's not my therapist. She takes off her glasses and god, she's gorgeous. I don't even care about the lipstick as I pull her toward me and start kissing her. I bend her over the desk and pull her pantyhose and panties down. Turns out, she moans. It's a sound I never tire of.

Neither of us regret it as she tries to fix herself back into the professional role. She repeats herself, saying how unlike her this is. She says normally her patients aren't this cute. She hands me her card before I leave, even though she's not my therapist anymore. Along with an SAA pamphlet and a list of meetings. I watch her as she straightens her skirt and pulls up her pantyhose. Maybe I am a sex addict. If I am, I don't think it's that bad. I give her a kiss goodbye and close the door behind me. Either way, sex addict or not, I don't really give a shit. There are much worse things in life you could be. The sex was phenomenal. Even if I don't get laid for the next two months, that session was worth it just in masturbating material alone.

FORTY-THREE

THE SEX ADDICTS Anonymous meeting is in the basement of a church and I rethink going inside once I get to the
parking lot. There are cars scattered in the lot, but not many.
I park my truck and get out, feeling weird about it. Selena
convinced me this would be good for me. Therapeutic, even.
To hear other people's stories, even if I don't share my own.
Against my own better judgment, I decided to listen and give
it a try. Even if it was more out of curiosity than anything.

Once I get inside and see the chairs in a circle I regret
stepping foot in here. It smells like disappointment and regret
in here and everyone looks so on edge. I'm wearing a hoodie
and I flip the hood up over my head and head straight for the
nearest empty chair I see. I avoid eye contact with anyone,
but I can feel eyes on me. Looking at me. Questioning. This
doesn't feel anonymous. My heart starts to race. The stench
of cheap coffee is filling the air.

"Want a cookie?" I hear a feminine voice ask.

I turn behind me to see where it came from. *Hello.*
There's a hot red head standing there. Petite. In shape. Her

tits are popping out of her shirt and I think she's evil for wearing that low-cut top to a sex addict meeting for people who are trying to sustain. My eyes fall to her nipples, because she isn't wearing a bra and in that lighting, I can very well see the outline of her round...

"Well?" she asks, wiggling the cookie in front of me with her hand.

I reach out and accept it. "Thanks," I say, with no emotion in my voice. I will not flirt with her. I will not look at her boobs. I will not...

"I'm Melissa. What's your name? I've never seen you here before."

"Names? I thought this was supposed to be anonymous."

She laughs. "It's anonymous because whatever we say in here stays in here."

"Gotcha."

She leans forward and whispers in my ear. "And whatever we *do* in here stays in here."

Oh boy. I grin without meaning to. I look at the clock on the wall. It's almost 7:45pm. The meeting starts at 8 and I'm already thinking of how many positions I can put her in within that fifteen minutes. When I look back at her she's looking at the clock, too.

Then she looks at me. "You smell like smoke. You got an extra cigarette?"

I nod. "I only have menthol."

"That's fine. Come on." She gets up and I follow. But she stops and turns around. "I need to use the bathroom first." She's smiling, suggestively. Looking at me with that look. I know that look.

"Okay," I say.

She tugs on the bottom of my shirt and lets out a soft moan only I can hear. "Meet me in the upstairs bathroom.

Wait two minutes before you leave. Take the back way or it'll be too obvious."

"Yes, ma'am." She lets go of my shirt and I watch her walk away. Her jeans are cupping her ass in the most beautiful way possible and I wonder how she even put those things on they're so tight.

I look at the clock, and I go outside to smoke real quick just to pass the time. And also so these random people can't watch my dick get hard in here.

A few minutes later I put out my cigarette and take the front entrance to the bathroom upstairs. When I get in the girls' room, she tells me to lock the door and leave the lights on.

She begs me not to use a condom, but I insist. I've never gotten head this great in a bathroom stall before. And I didn't know it was possible for a 5"1 red head to straddle you on a dirty toilet and make it seem so fucking glorious.

I never did hear the stories of the strangers downstairs. But I think they may have heard ours.

PART FIVE

NOW

FORTY-FOUR

THE ALARM SOUNDS in my ear, waking me from a deep sleep. I was dreaming of something, but I already forget what it was about or if it was any good. I roll out of bed, morning wood still in place. I have no idea which Vivienne to expect today but I decide to take care of myself beforehand just in case. You just can't go into a situation like that even the slightest bit sexually frustrated, or there is no hope for you. Or me, at least. Hell, there may be no hope for me anywhere. I'm starting to think that way. Maybe I just am who I am.

I turn the closet door knob in my hand and look at Sabrina, lying almost horizontally in the closet. Head propped against the right side of the wall. Empty eyes looking past me. I pick her up, gently, try to make sure her head doesn't bump any corners as I take her out. I don't know if it's because she cost me six grand or if it's because I'm starting to view her as something more than just an object. It's starting to feel like she's been here longer than the real women. Like they leave, but she doesn't.

I wonder if things would be different if she could kiss me back. If she could sometimes say no to me. If we could fight, fuck, and love like a real couple. I lay her down on the bed and this time, when I'm inside her, I look her in the eyes and pretend she is real. Afterwards, I clean us both up and put her back in the closet.

By the time I get out of the shower and drink my first cup of coffee, it's time to go. I know Vivienne will be waiting for me. Waiting for me to make her feel "useful" again. I only hope when I get there, she has clothes on. Her body is too hot. She's too beautiful. Too sweet. I don't know if I have it in me to say no to her. Maybe I could turn down the sex kitten version of her. But the other one? The real version of her? No. That Vivienne is fucking irresistible. That Vivienne needs to be touched.

I'm in my truck pulling into her driveway before I can come up with at least one logical reason to say no to her if she tries something. She opens the door before I ring the doorbell. And I know this is bad. The door swings open and she's standing there. Hardly any makeup on. T-shirt and jean shorts. Too short shorts. I don't think she's wearing a bra and I'm trying not to check and now her tits are pressed against my chest as she hugs me. Nope. No bra. Please, god. Let us pray.

She's saying things I don't hear as I try to stop my hands from traveling down to her ass. Fuck, she smells good. Her blonde hair is up in a ponytail and now she's smiling at me. Looking directly at me. I feel myself smile back without meaning to and she touches my face. Puts her finger right on my dimple and grins. It's over. I know it's over before I even cross the threshold and step foot in the house.

"I was thinking we could paint the guest bathroom today," she says, walking up the stairs ahead of me.

I'm trying to listen and not to look. But that ass. It's perfect. And now I want to bend her over right here on the stairs.

"I'm thinking a light teal blue," she continues. "I'll show you the color and you can tell me what you think."

She's making her way down the hallway now, with me trailing behind her. And we reach the bathroom. It's, it's too small. It's too fucking small. Too close quarters for just me and her.

She picks up the paint can. "It's called 'aqua love'." And she laughs. My god, she laughs in the cutest way possible and I'm a goner. Part of me wishes her husband would just come home already. Spare me the trouble. Save his marriage. Keep his beautiful wife. Aqua fucking love. Please, Vivienne, don't say love around me. It makes me uncomfortable in here. Now. With all the things I want to do to you. And I wonder if she would be happy if she were my wife instead. If she had chosen a different man. Someone who would make her laugh and smile like this. Maybe I am just new to her. Young. Something to take her mind off her misery. But hell, if it's a distraction she wants.

"Hand me that screwdriver?" she says. She's bent over now. Almost in a kneeling position by the paint can. She wants to open it. Maybe she wants to feel new, too. And I hand her the screwdriver and she pops the top open and fights back a smile. I can see the blush in her cheeks before she realizes it. But she feels me looking at her. Because she looks up at me. She's stirring the paint now. "What?" she asks, smiling.

I smile and shake my head. "Nothing," I say, casually leaning against the shower.

"Why are you looking at me like that?"

"Like what?" I ask.

She puts her lips together like she's biting something back. And she looks down. "Like I've been looking at you." She says it so softly I almost can't hear it. But I hear the pause in her voice. The shake. The embarrassment.

I wait for a minute, to see if she's going to say something else, to give her room to. But she doesn't. I don't move, but I finally speak. "You have thirty seconds to say anything else you've been wanting to say to me."

"I'm sorry," she says, quickly, standing up. "I didn't mean, I just..."

I take two steps toward her and lift her up by her waist and put her on the bathroom counter. "Don't you ever apologize again for something you shouldn't be sorry for." And I lift her legs up and wrap them around me and lean her back so her head is against the wall. I lean in closer and stop. If she wants this to happen, she needs to be ballsy enough to grab me and kiss me. And she does.

She pulls me into her and touches her lips to mine with a hunger I haven't felt in a while. She's pulling at my jeans and squeezing my arms and we are aqua love in this bathroom, on this counter. She stops kissing me only to pull her t-shirt off and fuck, her tits are perfect. And they're fake, but she's still real. My mouth moves toward them and I am kissing her all over her chest, her stomach, her thighs. I pull her shorts off and toss them to the side. Her legs are so smooth as I'm running my hands up both of them. And I start kissing the inside of her left thigh and she moans.

By the time I finish down there, she's already orgasmed. And when she calls me Albert I don't correct her. She's collecting her breath now, hair messy, bare chest heaving. She came so hard the second time she almost cried.

"Ugh," she says, eyes closed. "Holy fucking shit."

I laugh. "Are you okay?"

She opens her eyes and looks at me. "Okay? I'm more than okay. I haven't had an orgasm during sex in more than ten years."

"Ten years??" I manage, as I pull my shirt on. "How do you do it?"

"How do I do what?" she asks.

"Stay with someone who doesn't make you feel good."

"Oh," she says. I hand her shirt to her and she pulls it on. "Well, the whole not orgasming during sex thing isn't hard. I don't mind that. It's always been that way with us. But now, I'm lucky if I even get a real conversation. About something other than the kids, or the bills, or the house. The man used to at least talk to me."

"So, why do you do it?" I ask.

"Why do I do what?"

"Stay."

"Look at me, Alan. I'm 53 years old. I haven't worked in more than twenty years. Where am I gonna go?"

"No," I say, "you can always leave. Start fresh. You don't look 53. Plus, that isn't even that old. You're never too old to escape something that makes you miserable."

She laughs, but this time it's sarcastic. Disbelieving. Almost mocking, like she's the wise one here because of the age. "It's so easy for people to say that. I hear it all the time, trust me. And it's a lot easier said than done." She's pulling on her shorts as she says to me, "Just do yourself a favor, Alan. Don't marry someone you end up hating later. It gets lonely fast. There's nothing worse than being married on paper but being alone in reality."

She looks in the mirror and fixes her makeup. From the mirror, she looks at me. "You know the saddest thing? I don't regret what just happened in here. I don't even feel bad."

But I do.

She leaves to take a shower in the master bathroom. And I paint aqua love on the walls, alone.

FORTY-FIVE

I HAVEN'T SEEN Lindsay since the night I almost bashed Jay's face into the sidewalk. And I know she's been mad at me because I haven't heard from her either. That, or she was just done with entertaining the silly idea of "us".

Because let's face it, I'm the kind of guy a woman sees a future with for maybe a weekend or two. A fun few months if they're really hopeful. A spree of wild fucking and hair pulling. I'm not the kind of guy that women dream of marrying. I'm the guy they will occasionally think of in between fucking their husbands. It may not have been love we were making, but memories. Because sex is something you remember even when you wish you didn't.

I left Vivienne's the other day and gave her a kiss on the cheek. She walked me to my truck and said goodbye. I couldn't see her again. I told her I wouldn't be coming back, but I didn't need to. She knew that. Just like it was unnecessary when she told me she would still think of me. We both knew that, too. Some things don't need to be said but people say them anyway. I think we all just like torturing ourselves sometimes. Or maybe we just state the obvious and say things to fill the awkward spaces where the silences are no longer peaceful.

Either way, we both knew I wasn't coming back. And we both knew she would never leave her husband. Not like it mattered. Dating, for us, was never in the question. We both knew what this was before it even happened. There's no point in dressing "just sex" up in an outfit it was never meant to wear. And neither of us had it in us to pretend that anything that looked like love might come from this.

She tipped me two grand in cash on the way out and I took it without hesitation. It was in an envelope sealed without a kiss. Hush money. A few c-notes so I would keep her secret so she could keep her sad little life. Because even though she probably hates her husband, she hates the thought of being alone even more. And a part of me can understand that.

I drove away from that house feeling an emptiness I've only seen in Sabrina's eyes. I wondered if I was cracking. If I was lifeless now, too. If all the shit that's happened to me has piled up high enough to crack the foundation that was probably never solid to begin with.

When I got home I showered and washed my hands until my skin was raw. Afterwards, I fucked Sabrina in a way that was more like lovemaking than it was with Vivienne. And it wasn't weird. It was...nice.

Now here I sit. On the edge of the bed. Thinking of that. Thinking of the way Sabrina felt. How it somehow felt different. And I can't figure out why. I get up and walk to the closet. I want to see if I can feel that magic again. With Sabrina. I want to see if sex with her feels better than it did with Vivienne. Again.

My phone starts buzzing in my pocket as my hand is

outstretched for the closet door knob. I pull it out of my pocket and look at the screen. *Lindsay?* It's a text message.

"Hey, wanna get drinks tonight? :)"

I look at the closet door again before I reply. And for a moment I'm sorry, because I will always choose a real woman over Sabrina. "Sure, when?" I send back.

"I'll meet you at your place in 20?" she says.

"Cool with me," I type, and I know before I hit send that within 30 minutes we will be naked in my bed. I guess she doesn't hate me.

I look at my phone and see I have three other unopened texts. None are from Alice. No surprise there. Two from Jenny that I'll read later because that girl just won't quit even when she says she's done. One from a number I don't recognize that says "Hey you". That could be anyone. I don't answer any of them and put my phone on my dresser.

I have time for a quick shower, so I go to the bathroom and brush my teeth then jump in. By the time I'm out of the bathroom and dressed, I hear the knock on the door and know Lindsay is here. I open it before she has the chance to knock again. She looks as cute as ever, and she's smiling.

"Alan!" she says, jumping up on me and throwing her arms around me.

I pick her up by her legs and bury my face in her hair. "Lindsay!" I say in the same excited tone.

She laughs and slaps my arm. "Don't mock me!"

"How have you been?" I ask her as I put her down.

Disappointment flashes across her face so quickly I may have missed it if I wasn't looking for it. "Good. Just, you know. Dealing with the aftermath of everything and all of Jay's bullshit."

"You're still talking to him?"

"Not really. But he wouldn't leave me alone. He kept

texting me and I finally blocked his number. Then he started harassing me on social media. Facebook, Instagram, you name it, he was using it."

"I shoulda beat his ass," I say. "Still could, you know. Just say the word."

"No, it isn't worth it," she says. "I'm sure he'll get over it. Plus, I've blocked him on everything now."

"Guys like Jay never get over it."

"You might be right about that," she says.

"I definitely am." I walk into the kitchen. "You want something to drink? Coffee? Rum? Beer?"

"Rum and Coke sounds good," she says, hopping up onto the counter in the kitchen. "So what's new with you?" she asks.

Besides the housewife I just fucked and the sex doll in my closet you don't know about? "Nothing really, been working the last few days, so that's good," I say, while busying myself with getting the drinks out of the fridge. I make one for each of us. "Other than that, nothing really. What about you?"

"Nothing. Been thinking about you," she says, looking at me, smiling.

"Oh yeah?" I hand her a drink and she touches my hand as she takes it and nods. She's giving me the look. That look.

She takes a sip from her drink, still looking at me. I'll let her finish. Let her take another one. And she does. Her hair is covering part of her face and she doesn't care. She likes it, I can tell. I like it, too. I like the way her lips look after she swallows her rum and coke and then presses them together in a way that wants to say something but she's holding it back.

I take a big drink from mine and put it back on the counter then walk over to her. I spread her legs so I'm in between them and wrap them around me. "What have you been thinking?" I ask, as I move her hair and start kissing her neck. She tilts her head back and moans and it's the only answer I need. I lift her up and carry her into the bedroom where I toss her onto the bed. I smile at her and her cheeks are flushed. She's already breathing heavily and taking off her shirt before I make my way over to her. I watch her pant for a few minutes, slowly taking off my shoes. I let her take everything else off me.

By the time we finish, if there was any part of her that still hated me, it's gone. She's pressed up against me under the covers and her leg is thrown over me. She grabs my face and starts kissing me, deeply, tries to pull me into her like she's ready to go again. You will know you have satisfied a woman if she wants you inside of her right after you just left her. Because at that point, there is no satisfying that appetite for you. The entire expanse of her desire for you is something you could never completely fulfill but damn it, she needs you to try.

So thirty minutes later, I do.

And for the two and a half hours that Lindsay is with me in my bed, I forget about Sabrina. And I ask her if she'd like to stay the night. Because I don't think I want to be alone tonight, and because a real, warm body pressed up against mine feels a hell of a lot nicer than Sabrina's does.

FORTY-SIX

I WAKE up and Lindsay's body is no longer pressed against mine. She must have rolled over at some point during the night, but I'm not sure what time it was or when it happened that she subconsciously decided she didn't need to be close to me anymore. Though I am not surprised. Sadly, nothing surprises me anymore. I am unsure of exactly when the element of surprise was no longer real for me. When everything became so blended together that the disappointments became an expectant rather than a shock. But somewhere along the way, it happened.

Her blonde hair is showering my pillow and her arm is bent at the elbow, hand almost clutching the comforter. She looks peaceful when she sleeps and I wonder if I rest like that. If anyone has ever looked at me and thought I looked happy. Peaceful. Safe and sound while I was dreaming. I wonder if anyone has ever looked at me like I'm looking at her, thinking she looks so fucking beautiful even with her eyes closed. And I kind of understand what Vivienne said now, about not even feeling bad about it. Because I don't feel bad that I fucked Jay's girlfriend. And I don't feel bad that she's in my bed right now. Looking this cozy. This happy. I don't regret it. Not even a little bit.

I get up quietly so I don't wake her. And I hesitate to leave the room because if she opens the closet door she will see Sabrina but I don't think she will wake up. I hear a light snore coming from her. Not an annoying snore, just the sound of her breathing softly, but deeply. But I need coffee, and a cigarette. I walk lightly to the kitchen to put the coffee on then I go and brush my teeth. I wash my hands twice in between and remind myself I need to buy more liquid soap because it's getting low.

I make two cups of coffee and bring them both into the bedroom and put them on my nightstand. Her breathing has changed and her body has moved. She's in a different position and this is where the paranoia comes in. I didn't hear her get up. Could she have? Did she open the closet door? Did she see Sabrina? She would have said something. She couldn't pretend to be this calm right now. I light a cigarette and sip my coffee and tell myself to relax. She didn't see anything. She moves. And she makes a noise. Almost like a yawn but the opposite, because this is it. This is her waking up.

Her eyes start to move and finally her eyelids open and she looks at me.

"Morning beautiful," I say to her. And I smile a little.

"Good morning," she says, inching closer to me. She puts her arm around my waist and leans her face into my chest. "Do I smell coffee?"

"Yes you do. I made you a cup if you want it."

"Of course I want it," she says. She lets go of my chest and sits up, pulling the blankets up with her over her bare chest. A sign that she isn't completely comfortable with herself yet. Or maybe she just isn't comfortable with me.

Her small hands reach out and I hand her the mug. "Careful, it's hot," I say.

She takes it by the handle and takes a sip.

"I didn't know how you liked it," I say. "I put a little cream and sugar in."

"It's perfect. Thank you."

And there's a silence now. I don't think it's awkward, but I don't think it's completely right either. And suddenly I have no idea what we're doing. What I'm doing. What either of us want.

"How'd you sleep?" I ask, just to fill the gap.

"Great," she says, probably lying. I only think so because she shifts ever so slightly but in a way that is away from me.

"Is something wrong?"

"I told you last time I was here how I like my coffee," she says. And she says it in a way that is offended. Demanding. Irritated. Like I should have listened. Like I never listen to her.

"I'm sorry, I don't remember," I say. "How do you like it?"

Now she's embarrassed. "Sorry, I didn't mean to...it's fine..."

"No, if you told me, I should have remembered. I'm sorry. I can make you another cup if you want."

"No, it's fine. This is good. I swear." But she doesn't swear.

She isn't looking at me and she's looking at her mug probably wondering what she is doing here with me.

This is why it's easier to not let them stay. Because mornings will tell you everything. Mornings will tell you if you've made a mistake. Or, mornings will tell you that you want them to stay.

I'm half and half right now which means that it probably isn't good. And judging by her body language, it definitely isn't good. I want to soften the silence but I don't know how to reach her. I don't know what to say.

She lets me sweat a little longer. After a few minutes, she hands me her mug. "Here, can you take this?" she asks. "I need to pee."

I take the mug and mumble something about "yeah, sure". And she gets up, covering herself with her hands. Finds her clothes on the floor. She puts them on and I am uncomfortable for her. I am uncomfortable for both of us. She leaves the room and I have already finished my cigarette but I want another one just to have something to do so I light one.

When she comes back I am almost done with my coffee. The kind she apparently hates. And I don't know what to say or do so I say and do nothing.

"I'm sorry about the coffee thing," she says, climbing back into bed. "It was a whole thing with Jay. He never fucking remembered how I liked it. And he always got me coffee the way he liked it. For an entire year, it never changed. It's just a sore spot for me, I guess. I'm sorry."

"No, it's okay. I'm sorry I didn't remember. I want to be the kind of guy who remembers that sort of thing." And I do. I mean it. I want to be that guy. But I don't know if I can be that guy for her. Because if I was, I would have remembered.

She shrugs and tell me it's okay. And then she climbs on top of me and reminds me why she stayed over in the first place.

And afterwards, it doesn't feel good.

FORTY-SEVEN

LINDSAY DECIDES she wants to go out for drinks, even if it is at the bar that Jay works at. And because I'm a stupid asshole I say sure. Whatever she wants. Whatever she wants, I'll do it. That's always my motto.

The morning incident after the coffee faded into something we could both deal with and after we fucked, she was happy again. She wanted me again. She was calm, satisfied. For the time being, anyway.

It is Saturday night now and because she's young she feels like she has to go out and party. She has to spend her Saturday having fun and having drinks and taking shots and dancing and fixing her makeup in the bathroom or whatever it is girls do in there and I am just the man who is going to accompany her, this time. Still, I hold her hand throughout the bar as she makes her way for another shot. And there, I am very aware of all the nothing that I am to her.

She is five shots in and I am too sober for this. She wants to dance but I don't dance and she doesn't care that I don't dance. She pulls me along with her anyway. Onto the dance floor, outside onto the sidewalk, here in front of the bar. I don't want another shot, and I tell her.

"Oh, come on! It's Saturday night!" she says.

Saturday night may as well be Tuesday night for all I care. When she gets older, she will understand. But right now she's 22 and doesn't give a fuck and has to impress her friends on social media more than they think they can impress her.

She turns to me with big eyes. "Fireball?" she asks, wiggling her eyebrows.

"Whatever you want," I say. Because fireball is disgusting but I fucked up her coffee so she can give me fireball instead of Jack or Captain. I deserve this.

The bartender – who is not Jay – takes out two shot glasses and puts them in front of us. Slowly, he pours the fireball in each of them and I pay him. She lifts hers to her mouth, all smiles, saying "cheers" with her eyes and her lips when I feel it.

A hand grabs my ass. And I turn around, ready to swing on whoever it is if it's a guy and ready to politely apologize if it's a woman. When I turn around, there's a guy there. Shorter than me. Definitely gay.

"Meet me in the bathroom if she's not doing it for you," he whispers.

And I black out, I guess. Because the next thing I know I am on the sidewalk constrained by four men. And Lindsay is here and she's visibly upset. She's been crying. Why are there cops here?

"He's decided not to press charges," the one officer says. Me?

"The guy was gay. He's en route to the hospital right now by way of ambulance. They're pretty sure he'll be fine."

"Do you think this was a hate crime?" the officer says.

"The other guy doesn't seem to think so, but he's pretty banged up," the other cop says.

"I sure hope it wasn't. I'm getting really sick of these incidents."

I feel cold water on my face and then hands. "Alan, Alan."

I move my head to the side. "What? What is...?"

"Shh," she says. "We're gonna go home now."

"Are you sure he's...?"

"He's fine," Lindsay says.

I feel her hand lifting me up but I'm much bigger than she is. A cop helps her lift me. And the words "hate crime" are ringing in my ears. I would never hurt someone just for being gay. I wouldn't do that. I wouldn't.

"Let us give you two a ride home," he says.

She nods. I am a waste of time and space right now. I don't have anything to contribute as they stuff me in the backseat and take off. I am looking out the window wondering what is going on. What did I do? What happened? Is he really taking us home or is he taking me to jail?

We get dropped off at my apartment and Lindsay asks the cop to walk us up the stairs. I tell him it isn't necessary but he does it anyway. I wind up in my apartment in my bed and I drop onto it like a fucking rock.

"Are you sure you don't want a ride home, ma'am? Are you sure you feel safe here, with him?" I hear the officer ask.

I guess she says yes, because he leaves. I hear his footsteps echoing as he gets farther and farther away and finally the front door closes.

"What was that called?" she asks, pissed off.

My head is throbbing.

"What the fuck was that?" she asks again.

I have no idea what she's talking about. "What? What do you mean?"

"You beat the shit out of that guy for no reason. Just completely went off. Almost killed him. Why!?"

Almost killed him? "What are you talking about, Linds? Get in bed. Please."

"I can't sleep with someone who is basically a murderer."

"A murderer, Lindsay? Come on."

"Alan, you beat the shit out of that guy. Why? Was it because he was gay?"

And now I'm confused. "How'd you know he was gay?" I ask her. Did they know he grabbed my ass? Came on to me? Did he tell them?

"I heard the cop say he was," she says. "Do you hate gay people? Are you homophobic?"

"Jesus, no! Of course I'm not! I have friends who are gay. I've protected them from bullies. Are you serious right now?"

"It just doesn't make any sense!"

Of course it doesn't make sense to her. Because she doesn't know what happened. Yet here she is, judging away. Drawing conclusions from a few dots she picked up along the way. "If you think I'm that much of a scumbag that I would beat the shit out of someone just for being gay, then why are you even here?"

"You know what, you're right." She's standing now. Deciding whether she's right or I'm right but it looks like she thinks she is. Because she picks up her purse and puts it on her shoulder. "I would never be able to be with someone who is so violent. And you have serious anger issues, Alan. You should probably look into that."

"Yeah, you must be right. Because you know me so well." I get up out of bed and walk into the kitchen where I pour myself a shot. She follows me. I throw it back.

"What's that supposed to mean?" she asks.

"Exactly what I said. You *don't* know me that well. Hell, you don't really know me much at all. And you think you can just toss out accusations like that? That I'm homophobic? That I hate gay people? That I'm a murderer, for fuck's sake?"

"Look, I'm just trying to understand," she says.

And then I think about Fred and I wash my hands. Then I take another shot and light a cigarette. "I'm sorry, I think you should go."

"Fine," she says. And now she's walking toward the door.

I wait for her last words but they don't come. And that's fine with me. Because I don't need her to understand. I need her to go away.

FORTY-EIGHT

LINDSAY IS GONE and I am still standing in the kitchen. Still pouring myself shots and throwing them back. Still chain-smoking. Still thinking about tonight. I would have asked Lindsay how badly I hurt the guy if she would have given me some room to. If she would have just been a little softer about the whole situation.

I light another cigarette and hope he will be okay. I didn't mean to beat the shit out of him. I wish he never touched me. He should have never touched me. You can't just touch people like that without knowing what their triggers are. I put the cigarette out and wash my hands for what feels like ten minutes and I'm watching the water and soap go around and around and around the drain in the sink until it all disappears.

I rip my t-shirt off and then my jeans and I take a long, hot shower. I am scrubbing my body with the soap bar and I scrub until the last bit crumbles in my hands. It is never enough. I dry off and I tell myself that Lindsay is better off without me. That maybe I am better off without her. That this had to end at some point and it might as well have ended like this. I just wish she could still think of me sometimes and remember me as a good guy. Not as this violent homophobic piece of shit she thinks I am now.

And this is the problem. All of this. With people. With real, living, breathing people. They will never understand you. Could never understand you. Most won't take the time to try. Most will throw you away before they even have a chance to get to any of the layers underneath. I think I have layers. Maybe not. Maybe people aren't as fucked up as I am. Maybe they all are. Maybe everyone else thinks of themselves the same way I do. Maybe we all sit at home alone at night sometimes, wondering if anyone out there could ever really love us. Maybe all of us have night terrors and nightmares and fucking dread the future sometimes because after enough time, it all looks dim. If the past is any sort of foreshadowing for the future, I'm skeptical that things will ever get better. And how can they? How can they if we don't let them? How can they if we don't try? Fuck. I think I try. I want to try.

I want to be the kind of person someone wants to know. The kind of person someone could look up to one day. The kind of guy a girl wouldn't be ashamed to bring home to her parents. The kind of guy a smart, beautiful girl would look at and smile, and maybe even learn to love one day. I want to be better. I keep trying to kill the old me and he keeps sneaking back out. Like a bad dog who just won't learn new tricks because he's learned to love eating the garbage because he's been doing it for so long. For too long. Maybe I'm just meant to drink the toilet water and not the stuff from the bottle. Maybe this is how it's supposed to be. Maybe this life is just practice. And lessons. And next time I'll get it right. I'll do better.

I throw on a white t-shirt and shorts and get into bed. I

get out of bed. I get the bottle of Jack from the kitchen and bring it into my room. I am drinking from the bottle now. I am chain-smoking in bed. I just want to sleep but I can't stop thinking about tonight. I want to apologize to that guy. I want to apologize to Lindsay. I want to tell them all that I'm sorry. I want to tell them how fucking sorry I am.

It is 1am and I am fucking wasted. I look at the closet door. I know Sabrina is in there. In the darkness. Tucked away from the world. It isn't her fault she's fake. It isn't her fault she was born made of silicone, void of feeling and the capacity to love. It isn't her fault she was painted without a smile.

I get up and walk over to the closet. I open the door and find her inside where I've left her. Leaning, lonely. I lift her up and bend her at the legs and carry her over to my bed like I would do if she were my bride and not my doll. And I lift back the covers and lay her down on the sheets. I prop her head on the pillow and fix her dark hair for her. Her empty eyes are looking back at me as my empty eyes are looking at her. And I realize we are quite similar.

And then I climb into bed with her and lie down next to her. And I just want to feel good. And I kiss her mouth that can't kiss me back and it doesn't feel good. So I lift up her shirt and I grab her silicone breasts and put my mouth on them. I gently swirl my finger on her nipple and kiss her neck. I grab her boobs a little harder, both of them. And I climb on top of her.

I take off her top. I take off her skirt. I remove my clothes, too. I go down on her for the first time. And she can't feel it, but I can. And this feels as real as it can. I put her legs up over my shoulders and I push myself inside her and close my eyes.

When I finish, I clean us both up. I put her top and her skirt back on. And I tell her that I'm sorry. And I repeat it until I'm crying. Until I am crying so hard for so many reasons. Until I wear myself down and pass out.

And when I wake up, hungover and groggy, and embarrassed that I cried, Sabrina is still here. And she is not looking at me any differently.

But I see her now. And I realize I didn't even have to say sorry at all. Because she wouldn't have left me. No matter what I do, she will never leave me. For once, someone won't leave me. And that's real. Even if she isn't.

FORTY-NINE

I WAKE up for the second time and it's 11:30am and I still feel hungover. Water. That's what I need. I get up and head to the kitchen where I drink copious amounts of water to try to salvage what's left of my head. The part that isn't pounding. No. Bed is a better idea.

The good thing about not having a job sometimes is that on days where I feel like staying in bed and not moving, I can do just that. I get back under the covers and Sabrina is still there. This bed is big enough for two. And I make my way back under the covers and bury my face in the pillow for a moment. I feel like avoiding all contact with humans or the outside world. I vaguely remember falling asleep. Blacking out twice in one night, now that's a new low. Even for me.

I reach for my phone despite my urge to avoid everyone. I need to see if I need to do any damage control. I have three texts.

One is from Lindsay. "Hey...I'm really sorry. I don't think you're a scumbag. Please call me."

The next is from Jenny. Along with two others from her, unopened. "Hey."

"Can we talk?"

"Alan...please answer me."

The third is from a phone number I don't know. The one that sent me a message yesterday. "Hey you."

"Are you available yet? I've been waiting."

And I want to respond to all of them but it will only fuel the fires. Sabrina's presence has reminded me that there are no futures with some (real) women. Jenny and Lindsay being two of them. It didn't work. There is no point in trying again. And maybe none of us ever tried because what we had was never something worth fighting for. Sad, maybe. But sometimes that's the truth. Even when you want so badly to be in love. If it isn't there, it just isn't there. And there is no forcing it to come no matter how good the sex is.

The other texts, I look at. I read them, over and over.

"Hey you. Are you available yet? I've been waiting."

This shakes something inside of me but my head still hurts and I don't know if my brain can function well enough to place this. There's been so many women, and I'm trying to remember who said this. What this reference is. If I'm forgetting someone I shouldn't be.

Then I remember her big brown eyes. And I can picture her face as I'm leaving. As she's telling me not to sacrifice myself for women who don't appreciate me. Sam. Looking back, she was right. I should have never left her place that night to try to fix things with Alice. There was no fixing that. Even without Sam in the picture.

I text her back. "Hey yourself, beautiful. And actually, I am." Right before I hit send, I look at Sabrina. I feel an ounce of guilt creep in. Like I'm lying. To someone. I can't tell which one of us I feel like I'm lying to though. Sam, myself, or Sabrina. But Sabrina is fake and Sam is real. Sam can kiss me back. I can have conversations with her. I can hear her heart beat if I press my ear to her chest. I can't have any of that with Sabrina.

I hit the send button and get up to make coffee. I jump in the shower while it's brewing. I try to wash last night off me, but everything still reeks of regret.

I get out of the shower to find a new text message from Sam.

"Let's do this."

And involuntarily, I smile. She's cool. And I reply. "Let's."

A moment later my phone goes off.

"Time and place?"

And I stop smiling. I will not have sex with her. Not today. Not yet. I want this to be more than lust. I want to give something a chance without tainting it so quickly.

"The pier? Twenty minutes?" I send back.

"Deal!" she says. "See you soon."

I get dressed and kiss Sabrina on the forehead before I put her in the closet. Today is a day I will spend with a real woman. Sabrina will be here when I get back. I leave my apartment and head to the pier. I know I'll be early. But I should be. Sam is the kind of girl who should never have to wait for even a single moment.

As soon as I see her approaching, jeans and a flannel around her waist with a white t-shirt on, I smile. Something happens in my chest and the thing in there starts to constrict, starts to move. For some reason, I am nervous. Fuck, she's cute. Too cute. She smiles when she sees me. She's running toward me now.

"Alan!" she yells, sarcastically. Like she is in some romance movie and I am the love interest. And she's running slowly, but dramatically. Like she is in slow motion and the whole movie has been leading up to this very moment.

And I am laughing and I open my arms wide. "Adrienne!"

And she jumps into my arms and I pick her up and swing her. And she puts her hands on my face. "My whole life, I've spent it just waiting for this moment. To see you again."

I keep my face serious. "If you're a bird, I'm a bird."

And she starts cracking up. And my god, her laugh is contagious so I am laughing now, too. Her smile, breathtaking. I feel dumb. So dumb. For letting this girl go. For walking away from her once. I think about Sabrina in the closet and I look at Sam in front of me and I smell her perfume and listen to her breathe and Sabrina could never compare to this. And I shift while Sam is still in my arms. I look at her for a moment before I set her down.

"Hi," I say.

She smiles again. "Hi."

And just like that, hope grabs me by the throat and squeezes, and I feel like this is the beginning of something. The beginning of something real. With a woman who can kiss me back. With a woman I refuse to let go of. Maybe Sam doesn't know it yet, but I do. This is going to be something special. Something neither of us will ever want to walk away from.

FIFTY

SAM HOLDS my hand the entire day and by the time I get home, I miss the feeling of her warm skin against my own. Her laughter is still echoing in my ears and I crawl into bed, alone. She wanted to come. She wanted to. But this time, for the first time, I am not rushing. I want this to be more than just sex. I want this to be something we can hold onto. Something we can grow, together.

I lie in bed and my phone vibrates. I grab it like a teenage boy, excited. There are things moving in my stomach and I think this is what beginnings are supposed to feel like. It's a text from Sam.

"I miss you already," she says.

I smile because I miss her, too. And I tell her.

"Can't I just come over?" she asks.

And how am I supposed to say no to her? I text her my address. We've only been apart for two hours and I know we are both in trouble.

When you meet someone, that spark is either there or it is not. With us, it is there. It is impossible to ignore. It is an electricity you will either allow yourself to get shocked by or something you will run from. Something you will try to take cover from. Those of us who have been hurt the most, everything inside of us may scream to run. To escape. To get out now before you get hurt again. Some of us might stay. Some of us might stay because we are brave and some of us might stay because we like the hurt. Some of us might even welcome it. And some might try to deny it. But I won't. If this kills me, I hope it kills me slowly. I hope I feel every ounce of pleasure before the pain hits. And when it's done, I hope I die smiling.

I am brushing my teeth when I hear the knock on the door. I know it's Sam. And I run into my room and push Sabrina farther back into the closet and cover her with clothes and make sure the closet door is closed tight before I go to the front door to let Sam in.

I open the door and she is standing there, all loose brown hair and beauty. She jumps into my arms and kisses my cheek, my neck. She is whispering how cute I am, how much she missed me. How much fun she had today. How she wants a drink. How she wants to just get into bed with me and watch a movie.

I am smiling and moving my head because her kisses on my neck feel too good. Her lips are too soft. Her breath is too warm. Her hands are too full of magic. Her touch, too welcome.

And I kiss her back, but on the lips. And I am holding her face as I kiss her. Keeping my hands somewhere safe. I will not allow them to run along her breasts. I will not allow them to cup her ass or hoist her up onto the counter. I will be gentle and this will be different.

"What movie do you want to watch?" I ask her, as I pour her a drink.

"Hmm, what are our options?" she asks.

And I know she doesn't actually care. Neither of us do. I start rattling off movie titles of DVD's I own and when she decides on Green Street Hooligans I am happy. It's a good choice. And I put it in. And we climb into bed. She kicks off her shoes. I am sipping my drink and watching her in slow motion.

She is getting under the comforter now, squirming as she inches closer to me.

"Aren't you gonna get under the covers?" she asks.

I take another gulp of my drink and shake my head. "Nope." And I light a cigarette.

She sits up and looks at me, with a frown on her face. "Why the hell not?"

"Because," I say.

"Because why?"

"Because we aren't having sex tonight," I state.

She laughs. "Oh, is that so?"

"Yup."

"You've decided on that one?" she asks, grinning.

"Yup."

"And why is that?"

"Because."

"Any particular reason?"

I shake my head. "Not really. I just don't want to rush things."

"What if I do?" she asks.

"No means no."

She sighs and leans back. "Can we at least cuddle?" She wiggles her body closer to me and throws her leg over me.

"Oh no," I say. "I know what cuddling leads to. Get that leg off me."

"But..." and she is moving her body against me and her hand is on my thigh.

I gently move her hand. "Hands to yourself, young lady."

She stops and sits up, laughing. "Fine, let's *actually* watch the movie."

I grab her hand and kiss her on the lips. "Thank you. And it's not that I don't want you. I want you so much that I just don't want to ruin anything before we even get to know each other. Okay?"

She nods and kisses me back. "Okay. I'd really like to get to know you, too."

We don't watch the movie. We spend the entire time talking about our lives. She tells me how she's an artist. How she draws and paints and sells her work. She tells me how she grew up in a shitty neighborhood, in a piss poor apartment with parents who neglected her and made her feel worthless. She tells me how she has carried those feelings of abandonment with her. How she tries to leave people first so they can't leave her. I tell her I will never leave her. She begs me to stop her if she ever tries to leave me. I tell her I will.

She asks me about my life. I tell her about my mother's suicide. I tell her about my father. How we talk here and there now. She asks what happened with Alice. What the story was there. And I tell her everything. I tell her about Jenny. I tell her about Jay. I even tell her about Lindsay. I put everything on the table. Well, almost everything. I do not tell her about Sabrina. I do not tell her about Fred. I do not tell her anything that might drastically change her opinion of me. But I tell her enough. I let her decide if I am the asshole Alice told me I was.

And Sam decides I am not. She says Alice was wrong as

she kisses me and tells me she is sorry. She tells me I never deserved that. Any of it. She stops and grabs my face. She looks into my eyes. "You are worth loving, do you understand?" she says.

I stare back at her, unsure how to respond, because no one has ever said that to me before.

"You are worth loving and I am going to show you that, starting right now."

I don't know what to say so I grab her and kiss her. When I stop I rest my forehead against hers. "You are worth loving, too. Do you know that?"

We fall asleep with our clothes on. And we cuddle each other, and kiss, but nothing more. And in the morning, I wake up before her and watch her sleep. I listen to her light snore as the sunlight sneaks in to warm her. But when she finally opens her eyes, I see something in her eyes looking back at me, and it is not emptiness. I do not feel alone. And I have never known a more beautiful feeling.

FIFTY-ONE

WE WAITED three dates to have sex. Sam had said there was a three-date rule she read about in a magazine one time when she wasn't sure if she was a whore or not. She figured we could give it a try. Build some tension. Respect my boundaries. But she also said she wasn't a fan of rules. Whether it was one date, two dates, or fifteen dates, it didn't matter. To her, it was about the connection. The attraction. The thing that made her want to say *yes*.

And she said she felt that within the first hour of meeting me that night at the bar. That she felt it on the walk home. And that even then, it didn't feel too soon. I guess you could say I was never fond of rules either. Hell, I didn't even know there were any, really.

Today is our six-month anniversary and every day feels like a dream. Every day I wonder what I've done to deserve her. Every day I wonder why she puts up with my bullshit. I wonder if she's noticed the way I stink after I haven't showered in more than 24 hours. I wonder if she hates that I don't cook much. I wonder if she hates the stench of my cigarettes.

The smell of my morning breath. The way I can fall asleep mid-conversation on the phone, not because I'm not listening, but because I can just pass out within two seconds even if I don't feel that tired.

Last week she asked me why I wash my hands thirty times a day. I told her it was just something I do. No real reason behind it.

"There must be a reason," she had said. "No one washes their hands that many times a day without there being a reason for it."

"I guess I just like feeling clean," I said.

She pinched my cheek a little and said, "You're a weirdo. But you're my weirdo." And then she kissed me and asked what I wanted for dinner.

I think I loved her even more when she dropped it and changed the subject. Not because she wasn't still curious about it, but because she wasn't going to push. Because she isn't the type of woman who will force you to talk about something you don't want to. She gives me space to say what I want and keep in what I want and I never knew I needed that in a relationship. Sam, she just gets me.

I watch her making dinner in the kitchen and I smile. It feels right. She doesn't know it, but she is the one for me. She is it. I will ask her to marry me. Tonight. She tosses her brown hair over her shoulder and licks the spoon she's been stirring the sauce with.

My phone goes off and Sam checks it.

"Ugh, baby, it's Jenny again. Why don't you just answer her already? Please," she says.

"You don't understand, Sam. I keep telling you, Jenny is not the type to get a hint. Even if I tell her I have a girlfriend, she won't care. She didn't care last time. She won't care this time."

"Well ignoring her isn't going to make her go away. Maybe she just needs someone to talk to."

"She has her friends to talk to, Sam. I told her I couldn't talk to her anymore and blocked her, and she has texted and called me from three different numbers since then. Does that seem rational to you? I'm telling you, she just has this thing with me. She has never wanted to let me go and I don't know why. We never had a relationship."

"Well, still, I think you need to just call her back. Or text her. Something. She obviously is not going to stop until you talk to her." Then she stops talking and laughs to herself. "That reminds me. There was something I used to say to my brother whenever he was being a little shit like this to girls."

"Oh yeah, what's that?" I ask.

"Just grow a sac and call her back," she says. She can't even get the whole sentence out without bursting out laughing.

I walk over to the counter and grab my phone, smiling and shaking my head. "Fine. But it's our anniversary. Are you sure you want me to call her tonight? I can call her tomorrow. We both know she isn't going anywhere."

"How about your present to me can be calling her and explaining to her calmly that you have a serious girlfriend now who you are very happy with?"

"So the roses weren't enough?" I ask, and I'm smiling, because she has no idea that I'm going to propose to her. She has no idea about the ring in my pocket, the box grazing against my leg every time I shift.

She laughs and pushes me. "You're lucky you're cute. Go."

I grab her and kiss her and squeeze her ass while I do so. Then I take my phone and start to leave the kitchen.

"Hey," she says, leaning back against the counter and crossing her arms. "You can call her in here, you know."

"What? You don't trust me?" I ask.

"Of course I do. But I'm nosey. I want to hear the conversation. Put her on speaker."

"Isn't that a little mean?" I ask.

"No. Just let her know when she answers that she is on speaker phone and your girlfriend is in the room. This way, she knows. Then it isn't mean. It's just honest."

"Yeah, you're right. Okay. Wish me luck." I sit down at the kitchen table and open my phone.

Sam pours me a shot. "Here. You might need this. In case she cries or something."

I throw it back and open Jenny's last text message.

"Please call me. I really need to talk to you. Please."

I dial the number and she picks up before it can even ring a second time.

"Alan," she says.

"Hey, Jenny," I say.

"Where the fuck have you been? Why have you been ignoring me for so long?" she says. Her tone is angry. And rightfully so.

"I'm sorry, I didn't want to ignore you but I told you I didn't think we should talk anymore and I meant it. It's not good for either of us. And I've been seeing someone. I have a girlfriend. I think you're a..."

"I'm fucking pregnant, you asshole. It's yours."

Her voice echoes off the kitchen walls and I swear it's hanging somewhere in between Sam and me and the smell of the red sauce Sam makes for the pasta. Jenny hangs up on me before I can begin to process what she just said.

I am staring, avoiding looking at Sam. And all I can hear

are her words repeating themselves. *I'm fucking pregnant, you asshole. It's yours.*

You asshole.

Sam sits across from me, in a slow, shocked fashion, and pours me another shot. "So, there's that," she says. "Happy anniversary. Another woman is pregnant with your child." Then she holds the bottle up in mock cheers and takes a long swig straight from the bottle.

I throw the shot back and then get up and wash my hands. I am scrubbing them and hoping this all goes away but inside, and by the way Sam is staring blankly at the empty shot glass across from her, I know it won't.

FIFTY-TWO

I AM WASHING my hands for the fourth time when Sam puts her hand on my shoulder and asks if I'm okay.

I nod.

"You haven't left the sink since she hung up," Sam says, quietly.

I nod again. And I should be the one comforting her right now.

She reaches past me and turns off the faucet then grabs the dish cloth on my counter and dries my hands, gently. She holds them and looks up at me. I look away. I don't want to see the disappointment in her eyes. I don't want her to see the shame in mine.

"Hey, look at me," she says.

So I do. I force my eyes to meet hers and I don't know if I'm swallowing back puke or tears but something is caught in my throat or my eyes or my lungs or my chest and I don't know what it is or how it's going to come out and I am afraid. I am fucking scared. Sometimes things happen to you in your life. Shit fucking happens to you sometimes. Sometimes it is out of your control. Sometimes there is nothing you could have done differently to change it. It was just meant to happen to you. But this? This was not one of those things. This was something that was in my control. This could have been avoided. This didn't have to happen. And for what? 20-45 minutes of feeling good? Of getting off? Getting my dick sucked? It feels vulgar just to think about. And right now, sex does not seem appealing at all. Not even in the slightest. This does not feel good. Not at all.

I feel the cold sweat rush over my body like a wave. Like a punch in the throat. And right now, I don't know what I need to do first. Hug Sam, not hug her. Ask her if she's okay. Leave her alone. Let her leave. Ask her to stay. See if she hates me. See if she still loves me. Call Jenny. Say I'm sorry. Sorry for being such an asshole. Say sorry to Sam, sorry for the same things. Sorry for never being good enough. For never being the man they wanted. The man they deserved. The man who deserves them.

Yeah, sometimes you realize what a piece of shit you are. Sometimes you realize it at 10pm in your kitchen in your little apartment while a good woman is cooking you dinner. Sometimes you realize it when you're alone but you drink that realization away. Sometimes you realize it in the therapist's office after she calls you a sex addict but you still fuck her even though all you really wanted was help. Sometimes you realize it when enough people tell you to. Sometimes you realize it when you don't want to. Oftentimes you will fight it. But sometimes you will accept it.

That sometimes for me is right now. Here. In my kitchen. Sam holding my hands in the washcloth with her own wrapped around it. Tears in her eyes. Silently begging for me to talk to her. To say something. Anything.

"I am so sorry," I say. "I don't even..."

"No," she says. "It's okay. It was before me. I can't be mad. I don't have the right to be. I mean, obviously I feel a certain way. I feel a little bit of jealousy. Knowing she will have your child before I do. Knowing she will know what it feels like first. But, I can see the shock on your face. I know you haven't talked to her since we started seeing each other. I know you didn't cheat on me. I know this wasn't planned."

I am swallowing back that thing in my throat but it's getting bigger and I'm afraid it might just come up. Sam is so kind. Too kind. Too good. I don't know how she is so calm and understanding right now. She should be beating the shit out of me for getting another woman pregnant. "I didn't cheat on you. I would never. I wouldn't do..."

"I know, Alan. I know."

She pulls me in and hugs me. And I say I'm sorry once, twice, a thousand times. I lose count. She is still hugging me. I think she's crying because I can feel something wet touch my cheek and I don't think the tears belong to me but then again at this point I'm not really sure. We stay like that for some time. And Sam is whispering things to me. Telling me it will be okay. That hey, if the baby looks anything like me, they will be the cutest baby to ever live. Telling me she is not going anywhere. That this shit happens sometimes and as adults we all take this risk. That sometimes even when you're careful, pregnancy happens and babies sneak in there. She says maybe I have ninja sperm and maybe she needs to watch out. And it does the trick, because I laugh.

And when she looks at me and says, "Hey, it isn't the end of the world, okay?", I believe her.

I nod my head for probably the thousandth time tonight and I think this is when I stop shaking. "I need to call her back. I feel like such an asshole."

"You're not an asshole. You didn't know," Sam says.

"I would have if I had just answered her."

To this, she says nothing. Because it's true. Because for once, maybe for the only time in my life, I am right.

"You were right. I should have just answered her." I take another drink and I punch the counter. I do not want to be like my father. Maybe I am just like my father.

She leaves the room.

I am sitting at the kitchen table, still processing all this, when she comes back.

"Alan," Sam says.

I lift my head to her. I have no idea how long she's been gone.

"Now listen, I trust you, but I am going to ask you this just once. Just this one time, okay?"

I nod.

"When was the last time you slept with her?"

"Seven months ago? Maybe eight. I don't know. It was before we started dating. I swear to you. On everything."

She nods this time. "Okay. Have you slept with anyone else since we started dating?"

"No," I say. "I swear."

"You swear? Because if I ever find out your dick has been in anyone or anything else but me since we met, and you lied about it, I will not forgive you. I need you to know that. I can forgive a lot of things, but I can't forgive a liar."

And I think of Sabrina in the closet. And I think of how I fuck her when I get the urge to stray. To find new pussy. To find excitement. Adventure. Comfort. Something when Sam isn't around. And I feel the thing that's caught in my throat start to creep up again. And I should tell her. I should tell her. I should tell her how sick I am. How disgusting I am. But I can't. I wash my hands again. A doll doesn't count, right? A doll definitely doesn't count.

"Alan," she says. Her voice is full of distrust now. I can hear it. I can feel it. "Please, if you have cheated on me, please tell me. You told me that one night when you were drunk that you might be a sex addict. If you are, we can get you help. But I need to know. Please. Just tell me."

I finish washing my hands and I dry them and I look at her in her eyes. "There have been no other women. I promise. I am not that sick. I swear to you on my life."

She nods and pours herself another drink.

I look at her and see the tears in her eyes. A trace of doubt and disappointment is there and it almost kills me. I can't tell her about Sabrina. I just can't. She would never look at me the same. "I need to call Jenny back," I say.

She takes the shot and nods again. And then she leaves the room.

FIFTY-THREE

I HEAR a knock on the door and Sam and I both know it is Jenny before we even acknowledge the sound. I am walking to the front door to open it and this is awkward but it is necessary. It is just before 11pm. It is late. It is my six-month anniversary with Sam. And a woman who is pregnant with my child is knocking on my door while dinner is being kept on low so it doesn't get cold and I don't know what this life is anymore. I am a little drunk. I need to be. Although I need to be sober and coherent and Sam is a little drunk because she needs to be. But she isn't going to be a parent soon. I am.

I open the door and Jenny is standing there. Her face is fuller than before and so is her body. Her stomach, plump with child. My child. And I may be an asshole but I do not doubt that this child is mine. I am not that much of an asshole. I open the door for her and I take her arm to help her to the living room. I don't know what is appropriate and what isn't but I hug her and I tell her I'm sorry for being absent.

"Why didn't you tell me sooner?" I finally ask her.

She moves a stray strand of blonde out of her fresh face and looks at me. "I didn't want to tell you over text. I didn't think it was something to send in a bubble. Especially because you kept blocking me. I didn't know if you'd ever see it. And I needed to know that you did."

"I'm so sorry, Jenny. Really, I am. I should have been there. I wish you told me sooner."

"I would have if you gave me the chance," she says.

Sam almost enters the living room but stops at the doorway and leans against it.

"Jenny, this is Sam. My girlfriend," I say. "Sam, this is Jenny."

Sam walks over to us on the couch and Jenny stands up. "I'm so sorry, this is really awkward," Jenny says.

Sam smiles. She's trying to be strong. "No, don't be sorry at all. These things happen. I mean it is kind of awkward, but it is what it is. How have you been feeling?"

Jenny sits back down and smiles. "Thank you for being so understanding. I've been really good, actually. The pregnancy has been easy. No morning sickness, nothing. I didn't even really start showing until two months ago. Hell, I didn't know I was pregnant for almost two months."

"How?" I ask.

"I took plan B after we, yeah. I guess I didn't take it soon enough. When my period didn't come, I thought I just messed up my cycle. But nope. Surprise." She says it almost shocked but in a sarcastic, unsure way. And she smiles and laughs nervously.

And I hate myself because she's nervous. Because she is telling me this in front of my girlfriend. Because she should have been able to tell me privately. *It's yours, asshole.*

Sam nods her head. "It was nice meeting you. I'll let you

guys talk." And she leaves the room and heads toward the bedroom.

And I watch her leave. And my palms are sweating now. Because Sam is never in my room without me for more than a few minutes. And I think of Sabrina in the closet. And I look at Jenny and see her belly full with life. A life I put inside her. And all of this feels wrong and I think I'm going to be sick.

"I'm really sorry, Jenny. I am," I say. I don't know what else to say. So I just say that again.

"Don't be," she says, giving me a sympathetic smile. "I'm actually really happy about this. I never really knew I wanted a child until I found out I was pregnant. It was like, all of a sudden, things changed, and I accepted it. And, it doesn't feel like it's all that bad, you know?"

I nod. "Yeah. Well, that's good," I say. "Do you know, if it's um..."

"She's a girl," Jenny says. And when she says it, I see the happiness in her eyes. The excitement.

And I smile back. And I feel the tears behind my eyes. And I'm just happy she's a girl. That it's not a boy who might grow up to be just like me. And then I am filled with a sadness I can't explain. A knowing that no matter what I do, I will never be able to protect my little girl from men like me. And the sickness wants to come out again. Up my throat.

Jenny must notice the look on my face. The green of my skin. Because she stands up. "Look, I know it's a lot of information all at once. And it's late. I'm gonna go. Just, call me tomorrow if you want. Or don't. I really don't want child support or anything like that. I just wanted you to know you were having a child. My next doctor appointment is in two weeks. You can come if you want. But you don't have to. Just, let me know, okay?"

I nod. And I stand, too. "I will. And of course I'll come. I'm so sorry you've been doing this alone. You're right. I am an asshole."

"You're less of an asshole than you think," she says. And she hugs me. "Oddly enough, out of all the pieces of shit I've slept with, I'm really glad you're the father."

"Thanks, Jenny," I say. "Let me walk you outside."

When we get outside, I notice her cab is still there, waiting. Apparently she didn't know how long she'd be here. If she thought I would have just kicked her out within minutes. *It's yours, asshole.*

I hug her goodbye and walk her to the cab and open the door for her. I buckle her seatbelt over her. She lets me. It speaks volumes. "I'm sorry I haven't been here with you this whole time," I say, "but I'm here now. From this point on."

She hugs me. And I think she's crying. I feel something wet and warm roll down my cheek.

"Your girlfriend seems really nice," she says, when she lets me go.

"She is," I say. "And so are you." I wipe the tear from her eye.

"Are you scared?" she asks.

"A little."

"So am I."

"It's not the end of the world, you know?" I say.

And she smiles. "I know. Goodnight, Alan. I'll talk to you tomorrow."

I nod. "I'll call you in the morning."

And I close the cab door and I go back upstairs into my apartment. It's quiet. I don't see Sam in the kitchen or living room so I go into my bedroom.

When I enter, I feel the blood drain from my body.

Sabrina is on the floor. Like a lifeless piece of shit. Just sprawled out with her legs open in the last position I had her in.

Sam is sitting on the bed, eyes empty. Emptier than Sabrina's.

"What the fuck, Alan?" she says. And she says it so quietly I almost don't hear her over my own heart pounding.

"Sam," I start.

She stands up. She steps around Sabrina's body like she's walking around a corpse. "You said you weren't that sick. You said..."

"I said I haven't cheated on you. I haven't."

She makes it past Sabrina and rushes past me through the doorway and into the bathroom. I hear her vomiting. I hear the sink faucet turn on. And then I hear it shut off.

I go outside the bathroom door and I ask her if she's okay. The door opens, nearly knocking me over. "You said you weren't that sick. You swore. You promised."

"I meant it, Sam! I'm not that sick. I swear!" I say. I am pleading with her to just look at me.

"All I asked for was honesty. That was all. That was it. One thing, Alan. One fucking thing." She's putting her purse on her shoulder and I don't know what to say.

"Sam, please," I say. And I move toward her and she flinches. Her arms go up. In disgust? In terror? She is revolted. I can see it in her face. In the way she moves her body away from me.

"I'm sorry," she says. "I don't think I can do this."

And she reaches for the doorknob and I reach for the ring in my pocket. I graze the case with my finger and grip the box as I watch the doorknob turn in slow motion. I look at the clock on the oven in the kitchen. It's 11:47pm.

Who would have thought your whole life could be ruined

in a matter of 50 minutes? It is almost midnight on a Thursday when everything falls apart. For the last time.

FIFTY-FOUR

I DECIDE NOT to chase after Sam. I let her go. I let her go even though she made me promise I would try to stop her if she ever tried to leave. But I am not going to convince her to stay. Because if you have to try to convince someone to stay, it's already over.

And I will not try to convince her that I am not as sick as she thinks I am. Because maybe I am. And I look at Sabrina on the floor and I think this is all so cruel. And I feel sorry for her and I feel sorry for Sam and I feel sorry for myself and I feel sorry in general. And I want to break something. I want to try to make Sam stay even though she doesn't want to be here anymore. I want to ask her to find it in her heart to try to love me even though I'm sick because even though I'm sick, I love her.

But I pick Sabrina up off the floor. I fix her hair. For a long moment, I feel the urge to throw her. To burn her and get rid of her, and I feel so much regret that I didn't get rid of her sooner that all I feel is rage. It's the kind of regret that rips apart your stomach and makes you wish you were dead. My insides feel like they're trying to tear themselves into shreds, trying to kill every evil thing inside of me, and they don't know it yet, but I do – the bad things will never leave. They are part of me.

And eventually the rage turns into sadness. And eventually the sadness turns into drowning. And the drowning turns into downing shots which turns into drinking straight from the bottle and now I'm in bed with Sabrina. And I am wasted. And I am crying. And I am almost-numb but it is never numb enough. And I tuck Sabrina in under the covers with me and I put my arms around her and hug her and wish she was real. And I wish she was Sam but I accept the fact that she is not. She is not. But she is here. And I take the ring out of my pocket and I kneel down on the floor beside the bed.

I did not have the chance to propose to Sam, but I still have the chance to make this right. I can still try to save myself. And I have to, I'm going to be a father. I don't have a choice in that. But I have a choice in the kind of father I want to be. And I want to be the kind of father who teaches his daughter how to do what's right for *her*.

And I know now that I have to choose a different way. A new way. A new life. With Sabrina. It might not be normal and it might not be acceptable to anyone but it's what I want. What I need. I cannot, and will not, have a little girl and continue to hurt women the same way I have always been. I cannot, in good faith, raise a daughter and teach her what not to accept or allow and still go on with my old habits.

I look at Sabrina and take her silicone arm and lift it to me, then I open the box and remove the ring. I slide the one-carat princess cut ring on her left ring finger and look into her empty eyes.

And she is still here. And she will stay. And at least it's

something. At least it's permanence, without the pity. And I fall asleep, thinking I better get used to this. Because if I am being honest with myself, maybe I am addicted to sex, and maybe the sex leaves me feeling even emptier than before. Maybe real women are not capable of understanding me. Maybe they aren't willing to try. And it isn't their fault that I'm this way. Maybe I'm not willing to share all the bad things inside of me with someone else. Maybe this whole time I thought the one thing I was good at was being good in bed when really, I've just been good at pretending. I've been pretending for years. I've been pretending that sex feels good when really, it doesn't. The shame is too heavy and it never leaves the bed. It is always there. Inside of me. And then I stick it inside the women I sleep with.

And Sam is right – I am sick. But Sabrina doesn't mind.

PART SIX

ALWAYS

FIFTY-FIVE

I AM in a cold white room waiting for my daughter to be born into this world.

Jenny's stomach had grown by the day it seemed with a soft yet ferocious ambition until I got the phone call.

"It's time," she said.

I had kissed Sabrina goodbye. These days, I leave her on the bed.

It was 9:37pm when I got the phone call that Jenny's water broke. It was 9:53pm when I got to Jersey City Medical Center. It was 12:32am when they said Jenny was 5cm dilated. She was having contractions every 3 minutes. It was a blur after that. Jenny was squeezing my arm and sweating and cursing and begging them to let her push

There is a male nurse in the delivery room. His name is George and I think he sees the panic on my face because he keeps me calm. Tries to, anyway. I feel like I am more stressed than Jenny is and I am not the one who is about to deliver a child. I am sweating, and shaking, and nervous. And what if something goes wrong? Jenny is too young to die. What if there is something wrong with my daughter? What if she is born sick like me?

I think about the things I went through as a child and I grip the chair and wipe my face. I can't think about my daughter having to go through any of those things. A wave of nausea hits me and I want to puke or pass out. I want to beg Jenny to keep her inside of her. To keep her safe from this world. To keep her safe from me. I pray to whatever god is out there that my daughter is healthy. Physically and mentally. I pray that she is protected from evil men and evil women and everything unsafe in this world. I pray that she is happy. I pray she has her mother's soft and trusting heart.

Jenny's contractions are occurring every two minutes now. George is rushing around preparing for the birth but he is calm. The doctor comes in. They ask her if she is ready to push. George asks me if I want to watch my daughter enter the world. They are all so calm. Everyone is calm except for me and Jenny. We are sweaty and nervous and Jenny is breathing like a wild animal and I am pretending that I don't need to throw up as Jenny grips my arm.

"You'll be fine," I tell her. "You're gonna be a good mom."

She looks at me and nods. Blonde strands of hair are stuck to her face and she is breathing fast and I see terror in her eyes and she probably sees the same in mine.

"You're okay. You're gonna be okay. Are you ready?" I ask her, and I take her hand and hold it and squeeze.

She nods again.

"Squeeze my hand," I tell her. "I'll be right here, okay?"

"I need you to push Jenny," the doctor says. His head is between her legs and a surgical mask covers his nose and mouth.

And then there is counting. And grunting. And moaning. And yelling. And Jenny is pushing.

"The head is out," the doctor says.

George looks at me and nods toward him. I peek over the sheet covering Jenny's bent legs and I see the first glimpse of my daughter.

And it is not pretty. It is bloody but it is beautiful. And Jenny keeps pushing. Until I see dark hair, like mine. And she keeps pushing. Until I see shoulders. Until I see little tiny arms. Until I see a torso. Until I see little legs. Until I see feet.

And I let go of Jenny's hand when our baby is out and Jenny relaxes and throws her head back on the pillow and closes her eyes. And we hear crying. And I feel tears rolling down my cheeks. I don't mean to cry and I wipe my face before anyone notices. And they ask me to cut the umbilical cord and I do. And they clean my daughter up until she is no longer bloody and screaming. And George hands me my daughter and shakes my hand.

"Congratulations. She's gorgeous."

And I look at him. I am not ready to be a father. I am hardly a good man let alone a good enough man to raise a daughter.

He looks at me and leans in and quietly says, "Hey, things aren't always this scary. It'll get better. You'll see. You'll be a great father. Even if you don't think so right now." And he pats me on the back and smiles. And he goes over to Jenny.

And I look down at my daughter. *My daughter*. It feels so strange to say this in my head. I have a daughter now. She is right here, now. In my arms. Cuddled up in this soft blanket. Dark hair, just like mine. A tiny little angelic face.

I kiss her on her forehead and look down at her. "I will do

everything in my power to protect you and make sure you're safe. And happy. I promise."

And I hear Jenny's voice. "Alan, let me see her."

And I turn around and walk over to her. "Jenny, she's so beautiful."

She reaches out her hands and I hand her our daughter and sit on the edge of the bed. And I stare at Jenny staring at our baby.

"Have you thought of a name yet?" George asks.

And Jenny and I look at each other. And Jenny nods. Because she didn't know what she wanted for sure until she was born.

"Are you sure?" I ask her.

She nods again. "I'm sure."

I look at George. "Alyssa Rose Shaden."

He smiles. "That's a beautiful name. Congratulations to you both. She's perfect."

When he leaves the room, I look at Jenny and squeeze her hand. "Thank you."

She smiles and nods. And I think of my little sister I never got to meet. The baby girl my mother never got the chance to see. The little girl who never got the chance to live. Not even for an hour.

And I look at my daughter who now has her name. The name the world should have known.

And I realize that the love I never knew I was searching for this whole time is right here, in front of me, cradled in a pink little blanket. With ten perfect little fingers and toes. And dark hair, just like mine.

And this? This, without question, is real love.

For a second, she opens her eyes and looks at me. And her eyes look dark like mine. But not a regular dark. The color is not of this world.

A good friend once told me that you can be in this world and not of it, and that is what I want for my daughter. I want her to stay like this. Happy. Peaceful. Safe. Unmoved by anything that is not meant to move her. Yes, my Alyssa Rose Shaden will be in this world, but not of it.

EPILOGUE

ALYSSA ROSE RUNS around like she has no idea just how important she is. Like she has no idea she is the best thing that has ever happened to me, like she isn't the reason I wake up every morning. The reason why I go to work every day and sit in a stifling cubicle that was not built for me. Office jobs were never for me. Not until I had a little girl to support. Not until I had to show her that even when you're given an injury, or an obstacle, you work around it. You work through it.

Sabrina waits at home for me every night. And every night, she is there. And every morning, when the sun comes up, she is still there.

I have Aly on the weekends. She's with her mom during the week. But even during the week, Jenny lets me come over whenever I want. She knows about Sabrina. She knows about everything.

When we had a daughter, I had no choice but to tell her. I was sick of the secrets. I heard once that secrets keep you sick. And I just couldn't let that affect Alyssa. I was done. Done with the hiding. Done with the pretending.

It is tiring, to be someone you are not.

And Jenny responded unusually well. Whenever I need the touch of a real woman, whenever I need a real woman to kiss me back, she's there. Our relationship isn't normal, but it works. For both of us.

Sam wound up reaching out to me. She came to bring my sweatshirt back. She said she went into my closet looking for one, and found Sabrina hidden in there, tucked away. Buried, like all the other parts of me I tried for so long to hide and ignore. All the parts I kept from her. She didn't understand, but she didn't have to. She couldn't be with a liar. And that's exactly what I was. I lied to her. I lied to myself. I lied to everyone. I insisted she keep the sweatshirt. But I never told her about the ring, or the proposal she missed by a half hour.

Alyssa will be three soon. Not only is she walking, she's running. She has tea parties with Sabrina. And it isn't weird. Maybe she is sick like me. But I tell her every day just how okay that is.

She is in this world, but she is not of it. And neither am I. Nor do I want to be. Now, then, and always.

ACKNOWLEDGMENTS

I dragged so many people into doll holes with me so here goes.

Mom, thank you for being my rock. You haven't read this one yet but, I know once you get over the sex doll thing, you will love Alan as much as I do. I'm sorry I still haven't written something "happy" for you yet. Maybe one day.

Dad, for always listening to my book ideas and ramblings.

I love you both so much. Thank you for creating a monster.

My brothers, Tyler and Derek. For being the coolest, strangest brothers a girl could ever hope for. I love you guys.

Jen, Kat, I'm going to group you two spectacular weirdos together for a moment here just to say this: "Crop the gold nipples." You both searched endlessly with me, for many hours, on many nights, for photos for potential cover options. Combined we've probably seen enough doll heads and blow-up dolls to last us a lifetime. I regret nothing.

Jen, I will be forever grateful for you and your relentless

pursuit to make me do the things I have to even when I hate it. Your intense want for me (and others) to succeed, is just a glimpse into your goodness. (Careful now, your heart is showing.)

Kat, sometimes I think you really might hurt me. I torture you with my OCD, with needing everything to be exactly as I envision it, even when I have no idea what that is. And you just tolerate me so gracefully. Thank you for the perfect cover, yet again.

Thank you both for always being there for me, in all aspects of my life, even outside this crazy writing thing. I love you two to death.

Alicia, I don't even know where to start with you. Your belief in me moves me daily. Thank you for your friendship, and for everything I am failing to say here. I love you. I'll see you at Houlihans soon.

Anna, you gorgeous creature. Thank you for putting up with me. You are one of the most talented people I've ever encountered. I am so lucky to have you as a friend.

Caroline Kepnes, for your brilliance, kindness, and encouragement, and for being the example of the kind of writer I want to be. One day, we will meet at a mall.

Manoella, for always gifting me the space and time I need to do this. And for being one of the best people I've ever been lucky enough to know.

Davecat, for writing such a beautiful foreword. Watching the documentary "Guys and Dolls" is what inspired me to write this book, particularly you. Thank you for existing, for unknowingly gifting me Alan, for showing people everywhere they don't have to conform, and for your willingness to be a part of this project. One of my dreams while writing this was to have you write the foreword, and you made it happen. Thank you, over and over.

My co-workers that have since become family. Amber, Conor, Erin, Randi, Amadou, Regan, Alex, Nosh, Jess, Irina, David. Between all of you, you've watched doll porn to aid in my research, scrolled through photos and things you probably wish you could unsee, and were there for me in more ways than one. Thank you. District 13rd, represent. You all volunteered as tributes. I thank you. And I love you.

For the readers (turned friends) who were there even before the ARC's went out. Steph, Erika, I count on you two so much. Your opinions mean the world to me. Thank you for being the best and most beautiful of readers.

Diana, you may not have designed this cover but I never get through a book without you.

My best friends, Grace and Jen, for things that will never fit on one page. I love you.

Santhya, Chris, Scott, Crystal, Nikki, Luna, Ottis, Christy, Topher, Lourdes, Erende, Rose, Thom, Tad, Strazza, Anthony, Nasphoria, Ash, Dru, Ramona, Marilyn, Gae, Peggy, Stephanie, Phil, Tim, and Celina. Thank you.

And to my readers, I love you. Thank you for taking the time to read my work, for your kind messages, for humbling me repeatedly. And for making this all so worth it. Never stop being weird.

Christina Hart is an author, editor, and animal whisperer. She has a BA in Creative Writing and English with a specialization in fiction. Her four self-published poetry collections have all become bestsellers. They can be found online, along with her six novels. Traditional publications include The Chapstick Chick (Unknown Press) and The Father They Didn't Know (Penmen Review). In her spare time, she plays with other people's books while simultaneously driving them insane in the process. She hopes you will read her other books and/or hire her to edit yours. She also hates writing bios.

Email: christinakaylenhart@gmail.com
Facebook Reader Group: Hart's Heathens

MORE BY CHRISTINA HART

Poetry

Empty Hotel Rooms Meant for Us
Letting Go Is an Acquired Taste
There Is Beauty in the Bleeding
Don't Tell Me to Be Quiet
Our Water Graveyard

Novels

The Rosebush Series:
Lavender and Smoke
Woods and Ash
Rose and Dust

Fresh Skin
Synthetic Love

Novellas

Ruin Me: The Summer of Secrets, Part 1

Made in the USA
Middletown, DE
13 May 2021